THE
Unforgettable
What's His
Name

To find out more about
Paul Jennings and Craig Smith, visit:

www.pauljennings.com
www.craigsmithillustration.com

THE
Unforgettable
What's His Name

Paul Jennings
illustrated by **Craig Smith**

ALLEN&UNWIN
SYDNEY • MELBOURNE • AUCKLAND • LONDON

Allen & Unwin
83 Alexander Street
Crows Nest NSW 2065
Australia
Phone: (61 2) 8425 0100
Email: info@allenandunwin.com
Web: www.allenandunwin.com

Allen & Unwin – UK
Ormond House, 26–27 Boswell Street,
London WC1N 3JZ, UK
Phone: +44 (0) 20 8785 5995
Email: info@murdochbooks.co.uk
Web: www.murdochbooks.co.uk

A Cataloguing-in-Publication entry is available
from the National Library of Australia
www.trove.nla.gov.au
A catalogue record for this book is available from the British Library

ISBN (AUS) 978 1 76029 085 6
ISBN (UK) 978 1 74336 928 9

Cover and text design by Sandra Nobes
Set in 14 pt Wilke by Sandra Nobes
This book was printed in June 2016
by Hang Tai Printing Company Limited, China

1 3 5 7 9 10 8 6 4 2

TWO DAYS THAT CHANGED MY LIFE

Even before all this happened I had never been like the other kids.

I wanted to belong. Have friends. But I was scared and shy and lonely.

At lunchtime I sat on my own, trying not to be seen. I didn't talk to anyone. If I climbed a tree the kids would look up and not spot me. If I was hiding among the bins no one could find me. It was almost as if I was a bin and not a boy.

Horrible Gertag would say, 'Where's What's His Name?' And I would blush.

One weekend it worked. I got what I wanted. No one noticed me. No one even knew I was there.

On the First Day I blended in with things. Whether I wanted to or not.

But on the Second Day I changed. I mean, *really* changed.

THE FIRST DAY

1.

The two statues were exactly the same. The same boy with the same hair, the same face and the same lips. Yesterday there was only one statue. Someone must have copied him.

Each boy squirted water out of his mouth onto a little bowl on a rock.

I stood on the edge of the park looking at them. Everything was quiet. Just the way I liked it.

For some reason the statues made me sad. One of the stone boys almost seemed alive. As if there was someone inside trying to get out. The more I looked the more real he seemed. Once I thought that his eyes moved. But they couldn't have. He was just a fountain.

The reason I was there so early on Saturday morning was to get away from horrible Gertag.

She was coming for the
weekend. And if I went
home she would be there.
Mum wanted her to hang
out with me because she knew
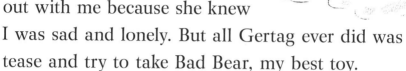
I was sad and lonely. But all Gertag ever did was
tease and try to take Bad Bear, my best toy.

And she called me 'What's His Name'. I hated
that. I really hated it.

Suddenly the thought was knocked out of my
mind. A noise filled the air. A loud noise. A scary
noise. At first I didn't know what it was. But then
I saw them.

Motorbikes. It was a gang of bikies. They roared
down the street towards me. They had black
helmets. And tattoos. And beards. And earrings.

They were rough and tough. And looked mean.

The bikies were all different. But in a way they were all the same. They belonged to the same gang. They obeyed the same rules. They stuck together.

No one could say a thing to a bikie. Everyone knows that. I felt a little tingle run up my spine. I shivered. What if the bikies looked at me?

I started to pant. I went cold. Then hot. It was like I was drowning. I couldn't get enough air. What was happening to me? I wanted to run away but my shoes seemed to be nailed to the ground.

I pressed myself into a bush next to the two statues. I screwed up my eyes. I pretended I wasn't there.

The bikies passed by slowly, engines growling.

'Please don't look at me,' I said under my breath.

They didn't. Not even one glance.

I looked down. And screamed.

I was GREEN. As GREEN as GRASS. My hands were GREEN. My skin was GREEN.

The bikies disappeared around the corner. The sound of their engines faded away. I was safe.

But I was GREEN. My clothes, my shoes. Everything. I couldn't believe it. No wonder the bikies didn't see me. I had blended in with the bush.

'This isn't happening,' I said to myself. I felt like an idiot. But the bikies were gone and I began to relax. I felt a tingling in my body. I looked down.

The green colour was starting to wash away. It was like a wave running out on the beach. I watched it sweep down my body and then it was gone. I was my old self again.

I looked at my hand. It was the colour of skin. Normal.

'Don't be stupid,' I whispered. 'That did not happen.'

I hit my head with my hand as if to knock the silly idea out of my brain. I started to walk along the footpath, thinking about my weird life.

A loud noise made me jump.

'Ruff, ruff, ruff, ruff.'

It was a big, sand-coloured dog. It had no ears and was wagging its tail. One eye was blue and the other one was brown. I held out my hand and the dog began to lick it. He liked me.

'Where's your collar, boy?' I said. 'Where's your tag?' He didn't have a name.

He was What's His Name. Just like Gertag called me.

At school I didn't want to be different so I pretended to be like all the other kids. If they ran I ran. If they wore red socks I wore red socks. If they ate Burp Bombs I ate Burp Bombs. But I didn't burp and laugh afterwards like they did.

In class, I never put my hand up. I just sat up the back daydreaming about my father. And wondering where he was. And what he looked like. And if he loved me.

The dog was a loner too. I wished he was mine. I made up a name for him.

'Good boy, Sandy,' I said. 'Good boy.'

I gave him a pat and walked away from the park. Sandy ran along after me.

I knew I would be in trouble if I took him with me. Mum went crook last time I went home with a stray dog. She said we already had two mouths to feed and that was enough.

'Go home, boy,' I said.

I yelled and shouted at Sandy but he just kept following me. I didn't really care. Everyone

was out with their friends. I was all alone. Sandy
made me feel more normal.

After a bit I came to the pub.

And there they were. Lined up in a row.

Motorbikes.

About thirty of them.

The bikies had parked their bikes on the footpath and gone inside.

I peeped in the window. The bikies were all talking loudly and laughing. They sure looked tough. Each one wore a black leather jacket with their name on it. There was a group near the window. I screwed up my eyes and tried to read the names.

The biggest was **THE CHIEF**. He was talking to a skinny bloke called **SHARK**. There was another one named **METAL MOUTH** who kept grinning and showing off a big silver tooth. Next to him was **MAGGOT**. He had a sort of lopsided smile and did a lot of listening but not much talking. They wore badges and studs on their jackets. All of them had beards and tattoos of snakes and skulls and other creepy things.

None of them were looking out of the window.

I stared at the motorbikes. They were black and silver and shiny. They sparkled in the sun. One long row of mean machines.

There was a sign on one of them. It said:

DO NOT TOUCH THE BIKES

I wanted to touch one. They were wonderful. They were marvellous. They seemed to talk to me.

'Touch me, touch me, touch me.'

I could hear the gang inside the pub. The noise seemed to grow louder and louder. There was yelling and shouting and laughing.

I heard the sound of glass breaking. Maybe a fight was starting.

No one knew that I was outside looking at the bikes.

I held out my hand. I reached out with one finger. I touched the first bike. A Harley-Davidson. It felt so good. So smooth. So powerful.

But then... but then...

It moved. It moved and jiggled. Just a little bit. I pulled my hand away as if I had touched a flame.

Too late.

No, no, no.

The motorbike fell.

Crash.

It fell onto the second bike.

The second bike fell onto the third bike.

The third bike fell...

One after the other they fell onto each other. Crash, crash, crash, crash, crash, crash.

Every bike was on the ground. All thirty of them. Some were scratched and dented. One had a mangled mirror. A light globe swam in a little lake of broken glass.

No, no, no. What had I done?

I looked up. A face glared out of the window. It was Metal Mouth. He was staring straight at me and Sandy.

Sandy jumped around barking with joy. He was having fun.

'Shh,' I said.

Another face appeared at the window. It was Shark. He pointed his finger straight at us.

'Catch him,' he yelled. I turned and ran. Sandy ran after me. He thought it was a game.

I heard voices.

'He's getting away.'

'Grab him.'

'Quick.'

They were after us.

I ran.

And ran.

And ran.

Behind me I heard the sound of engines. The motorbikes growled and spat and sputtered into life. The shouts of the bikies were drowned by crackling engines.

People in the street stopped and stared. Cars screeched to a stop as they gave way to the roaring machines. A kid fell off his skateboard. People backed into shops to escape the din.

I raced down the street as fast as I could go. I had to get away from the bikies. I looked around for somewhere to hide. Anywhere to be alone. To be safe. To be unseen.

I ran along the footpath with Sandy following. He was loving it. The road was wide and the bikies were sweeping down like a black river. They would catch me at any moment.

I ran as hard as I could.

I reached the main street. As I ran my reflection also ran in the shop windows. Something weird was going on. I was filled with fear. I started to pant. I went cold. Then hot. It was like I was drowning. I couldn't get enough air. I stopped outside the barber's shop and looked at myself. It was me and it wasn't me. I couldn't believe what was happening.

'Aargh,' I yelled.

I was covered in red and white stripes like the barber's pole.

Behind me I heard the terrible roar of motorbikes. I ran on.

The colours of my clothes and skin changed as I went along. I seemed to be blending in with my surroundings. Flickering pictures danced on my clothes and skin.

This was terrible. Horrible. I was a freak. I didn't know which was worse – being caught by the bikies or blending in with the background. As I ran on I kept changing. Once my clothes were

covered in pictures of little fairies the same as those in a dress shop.

Next I blended with a shelf of pies and cakes.

Then I blended with a display of shop dummies. And dead fish.

And… and… it just went on and on. I must have been hard to see, but not invisible.

I kept hoping that I would wake up. That this was a dreadful dream. A nightmare.

But everything told me that I was still in the real world. The smell of the fish in the shop. The small stone in my shoe. The shiver that ran up my arms. All of these things were real. You don't get them in dreams.

Sandy didn't like it. He gave a yelp and ran down a lane.

I heard the sound of the bikes slowing. I heard their engines rumbling. I screamed and pressed myself against a brick wall. I closed my eyes.

'He's here somewhere,' said a voice.

The engines continued to rumble. Then the noise grew louder and I heard them move off. They hadn't seen me. Why? Why? Why? Oh, no.

Now my clothes and skin seemed to be painted like rows of bricks.

I ran even faster until I was past the shops and surrounded by houses and open grassland. In the distance I could see a group of high trees. A head was peering over the top. Way up high. It was chewing. On leaves. I knew at once what it was.

A giraffe.

I stopped to catch my breath and examined myself. I was back to normal. The crazy images had gone from my body. But behind me I could hear the motorbikes. They were coming, they were coming, they were coming. I ran on, clutching my aching sides.

I needed somewhere to hide.

And I knew just the place.

2.

I had been to the zoo hundreds of times. Kids got in free if they were with an adult. Mum took me there all the time to fill in a weekend when I was feeling lonely.

I staggered up to the gate of the zoo and saw a man and woman and three kids walking in. I tagged on behind and followed them through.

The gatekeeper didn't say a thing. She thought I was part of the happy family. I was in. And I was safe. That's what I thought anyway.

'Oy,' shouted a voice. It was the gatekeeper. 'You can't bring a dog in here.'

Oh, no, Sandy had followed me in.

'Scat,' I said. 'Shoo.' Sandy's tail drooped. He saw the keeper coming and started running down a path.

I went belting after him but he crawled through a hole in a fence and disappeared. I stopped outside a building that had a picture of a lizard on the wall. The sign said:

REPTILE HOUSE

It brought something to mind. Something very interesting.

I was thinking about some lizards I had heard about. They changed colour to fit in with the background. It was how they hid from birds and snakes. They didn't want to be noticed. Like me.

What were they called? Think, think, think.

Chameleons. Yes, that was it. Something told me to go and check them out.

It was warm and dark inside the reptile house. There was a long passage with windows on each side. I walked slowly, looking into each window.

Snakes. I gave a shudder. There were five or six different types. And crocodiles. And alligators.

And all sorts of lizards: frill-necked, blue-tongues and many more. Finally I came to a window with the word I was looking for in big letters on the wall next to it.

CHAMELEONS

At last. I stared through the glass. There were a lot of tree trunks and twisted branches. But nothing moved. There were no chameleons.

'What a pain,' I said under my breath. 'I came in here for nothing.'

I looked into the glass cage again. There was not one chameleon to be seen.

Or was there?

Of course.

Why didn't I think of it?

They were all hiding. They were wearing their camouflage. I looked more carefully.

Yes. There was one on a branch. I could see the outline of its body. It looked like a piece of bark. But I could just make out legs and the shape of its tail.

And there was another one among some leaves. It was green and had bulging eyes. Each eye looked in a different direction. They were weird, like two marbles rolling around in bowls.

A terrible thought entered my mind. What if I got stuck when I was green or some other colour? What if I couldn't change back? What if I stayed blended with a tree for ever? Or a brick wall? Or something worse?

I wanted Mum. I had to get home where I would be safe.

I peered at the chameleon with the rolling eyes. A long tongue shot out and caught a fly.

Boy, I was glad I wasn't a chameleon. I did have a long tongue myself. But I would never eat flies. Yuck.

I decided to get out of the zoo. There was nothing there that made me feel better.

I stepped out of the passage into the sunlight and found Sandy sitting waiting for me. There were no keepers in sight.

'Where have you been, Sandy?' I said. 'Come on. Quick, we have to get out of here before they catch you.'

At that very moment I heard a yell.

It was Shark.

'There he is,' he shouted.

They were after me. The terrible bikies. I could see black helmets and bristling beards bobbing around all over the zoo. I couldn't let them catch me.

I looked around for somewhere to hide. Somewhere. Anywhere. They were coming, they were coming, they were coming.

3.

Nearby, a man and a woman were unloading some big plants out of a truck.

Sandy was yapping and wagging his tail.

'Shoo,' I whispered. He gave a friendly yelp. One of the bikies heard him. It was Metal Mouth.

'There he goes,' he yelled.

I heard the sound of heavy boots running right behind me.

The nursery people were getting ready to take the plants into the monkey cage. They had unloaded some trees that were big enough for the monkeys to climb and hide in. I jumped into the middle of them and stood still. Sandy followed me.

'Shoo,' I said again. This time Sandy slunk off with his tail between his legs. Poor old Sandy. If he had ears he probably would have flattened them. I felt sorry for him but I couldn't let the bikies catch me.

Once again I heard Shark's voice.

'He's around here somewhere.'

I could hear the bikies searching, searching, searching. They were getting closer. I tried not to think about their broken bikes. And how angry they were.

Next to the plants was a forklift truck. In front of it was a very large tree in a pot. Big enough to climb. I scrambled up onto the pot but before I could climb into the tree I heard a shout.

I pressed myself against the trunk of the tree. I started to pant. I went cold. Then hot. It was like I was drowning. I couldn't get enough air.

I looked down. Oh, no, no, no, no, no. What had happened?

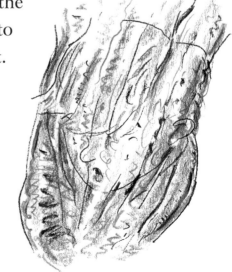

My legs had changed. They looked like roots going into the pot plant. My feet seemed to be buried in the dirt.

My arms were like vines twisting around the trunk. I couldn't see my face but my mouth felt like a little pouting knothole. I had blended into the tree. I was a boy with skin that looked like bark.

The nursery man put down the small pot plant he was carrying and stared at me. Then he shouted out.

'Violet, come and look at this.'

His wife walked over and they both peered at me.

'This tree looks like it's got a face,' he said to Violet.

'Amazing,' she said. 'It does too. If you squint you can see a sort of frightened face. I've never seen anything like it before.'

'It's suffering,' the man said. 'It needs water.'

He bent down and picked up a hose.

'We don't want it to die,' he said. He pointed the hose at me and gave me a good soaking. I copped it everywhere. Even in my face.

'I'll get some manure for it,' said his wife. 'The poor tree is in shock. It needs some liquid fertiliser.'

'It could be worth big money,' said the nursery man. 'We could take cuttings, and plant more back home. Everyone will want a tree with a face.'

They both started to laugh. But I didn't think it was funny.

Cuttings. What if they took a bit of me? What if they thought my finger was a twig and cut it off?

I had another thought. Liquid fertiliser. I didn't like the sound of that either.

Violet went over to the van and came back with a watering can. I could smell it before she even got near me.

She started to pour a foul brown liquid all over my feet. She was fertilising me.

'It's elephant poo,' she said. 'Mixed with a bit of monkey. Nice and fresh.'

'Pour some on the leaves,' said the nursery man. 'It can drip down slowly.'

Violet poured the stinking stuff higher up the tree. It dribbled down all over me. I felt as if I was going to vomit.

The nursery man took out some clippers and reached up high. He started to chop away at the leaves. It hurt my head. Like when the barber tugs your hair.

'That's enough,' said Violet. 'Don't prune it too hard.'

The nursery man held a bunch of twigs and leaves. He put them in the back of the truck. I could hear him talking.

'We'll make a mint if we can grow another one,' he said.

Just then I heard another voice.

'I know he's around here somewhere.'

It was The Chief. He had a deep booming voice. He looked up at me but didn't say anything.

'I'll check these plants,' said Metal Mouth. His teeth clicked as he talked. It sounded like a knife hitting a fork. He started to push over the pot plants. Some of them rolled over and dirt spilled out of their pots.

'Hey,' yelled the nursery man. 'Stop that.'

The bikies gathered around him.

'Stop what?' said The Chief in a tough voice.

The nursery man looked at their faces and fell silent.

'Sorry, mate,' said Maggot. I noticed that he had a broken-heart tattoo on his shoulder. On one side it had the word *Maggot* and on the other half it said *Firebird*. Underneath it had an eye with tears dripping out of it.

The bikies kept on pushing through the spiky plants. Maggot followed the others, picking up the knocked-over pots and standing them the right way up.

'He's here somewhere,' said Metal Mouth.

'Hey, this tree is weird,' growled Shark.

The gang came over and took a look at me.

'It's sort of got a face,' said Maggot.

They all stared. So did the nursery man. Metal Mouth scoffed. His silver tooth twinkled in the sunlight.

'Don't be stupid,' he said. 'Plants don't have faces.'

Maggot peered at me. He gave a friendly smile. 'I like it,' he said.

'How much?' Shark said to the nursery man.

'Not for sale,' he said. 'It belongs to the zoo.'

Shark was not happy.

'My old granny would like that tree,' he said. 'She's getting on a bit. She would love a tree that has a face on it. It might cheer her up.'

'Not for sale,' the nursery man said again.

Shark frowned.

'I want that plant,' he said.

'No time for that now,' said The Chief. 'Spread out. Search the whole zoo, we need to find him.'

They all started to move off. Shark was still

grumbling under his breath. 'Poor old lady. That tree would make her laugh.'

My heart stopped its pounding. I started to feel safe again. I was out of danger. For now at least.

But that didn't last long. Violet walked over to the gate of the monkey pen and pressed some buttons. The gate swung open. Her husband lifted a pot onto a trolley and wheeled it through the gate. Violet quickly slammed it shut after him.

'You have to be quick,' she said. 'So the monkeys don't get out.'

They were moving all the plants into the monkey cage. One by one they wheeled them in. Soon the only plant left outside was the huge tree with the face. My face.

'It seems a pity to let the zoo have it,' said Violet.

'We have to,' said her husband. 'The zoo has paid for all these plants.'

He started up the engine of the forklift truck and lifted me and the pot and the tree into the air.

Then he drove forward and into the monkey cage. He pulled a lever and dumped the pot on the ground. He looked at me one more time, shook

his head and drove out. Violet slammed the gate
closed.

The nursery man drove the forklift up a ramp
and onto the back of his truck. Then they both
drove off. I was alone.

Trapped inside with the monkeys.

The monkeys walked around the new pot plants that were spread through their pen. At first they didn't seem to like them. The monkeys pulled their lips back over yellow teeth and started to spit and howl and jump around.

One monkey was bigger than all the others. He did an angry dance and waved his long arms at me. A horrible screeching noise burst out of his mouth. His teeth were sharp and cruel.

I could see that he was the boss monkey.

He climbed up onto my pot, lifted a leg and let fly with a squirt of pee. It splashed all over my bark. I couldn't believe it. He had taken a leak on me. Just like a dog. It reminded me of Sandy. I was all wet and miserable.

The other monkeys came to life. They chattered and squeaked. They seemed to be laughing.

I realised with a shock that everything was okay. The boss monkey had peed on me. It was a sign. He liked the new plants. So he must have liked me. That made me feel a bit better. Even though the pee was stinky.

The other monkeys scampered over and climbed into the branches above my head. My tree was their favourite plant.

After a bit I heard footsteps at the gate. Two keepers appeared.

I heard a voice. 'What's the passcode again?'

'One, two, three, four.'

The first keeper laughed. 'Too easy.'

'Monkeys can't count,' said the other voice.

I heard four beeps and then saw the gate swing open. The keepers entered and tipped up a bin full of bananas.

The monkeys swarmed over the pile. They started to grab the bananas with greedy fingers and gobble them up. There was much squealing and shrieking and fighting.

The keepers quickly moved out through the gate while the monkeys fought over the food.

There was one very small monkey who wasn't getting any bananas. He squatted down watching his brothers and sisters with sad eyes. He was on the edge of things. Left out of it. He reminded me of myself at school.

Suddenly the big monkey opened his mouth and shrieked. He walked slowly to the pile of bananas and started to eat while the others watched. He was the boss all right. The Big Pee.

He gobbled banana after banana while the others stood there licking their lips. Finally he couldn't fit any more in. He gave a loud belch and patted his swollen stomach.

This was the sign for the others to go back to eating. And fighting. The little monkey still watched hungrily. He didn't even get one banana.

Finally every banana was eaten. The tribe started to fall asleep. One by one they dozed off for an after-lunch nap. The Big Pee was the last to close his eyes.

I stood there on the pot and pressed myself back onto the tree. I was still covered in bark, with arms and legs that looked like vines and roots.

The Big Pee had put his mark on me. I smelled of monkey. The others in the tribe had accepted me. And now they were all asleep. I was still in trouble. Cold, hungry and looking like part of a tree. But I felt a little better because at least the monkeys were not going to hurt me.

At that very moment my covering of bark started to swirl and move and fade away. In no time I was myself again. I stepped off the pot. The tree looked just like it had before. No sign of a face.

I took a step towards the locked gate.

And sensed that eyes were watching me.

It was the little monkey. He looked at me with hopeful eyes. What did he want? Friendship? Freedom? Food? Maybe all three.

'What's your name?' I whispered. He didn't answer of course.

'You've got to have a name. I'll call you Banana Boy,' I said. 'One day you will have all the bananas you want.'

I didn't know why I said that. It just came out.

I felt around in my pocket. A Burp Bomb. My favourite lolly.

I peeled off the wrapper and gave it to the little monkey. He took it with a shaking hand and put it in his mouth. He chewed it hungrily. I could see that he loved it. He gave one big swallow and patted his stomach.

Then he gave a little burp. Just like the kids at school.

I laughed. In the middle of all my troubles I could still laugh. It was a lovely moment. We were mates. Me and the monkey.

Sandy was my mate too. But where was he?

I had to find him. He had no collar and that made him a stray. Anything could happen to a stray.

I crept over to the gate. There was no one around. No sign of the bikies. In the distance I could hear a crowd cheering. I knew what it was. Feeding time for the seals. Everyone loved it when the keepers threw fish into the water and the seals dived for them.

I pressed the buttons: 1, 2, 3, 4.

The gate swung open and I jumped out. I was free.

Banana Boy gave a little squeak. And then...

No, no. He jumped out after me. Oh, what?

Big Pee opened one eye. And then the other. He saw what was going on. He followed. And so did all the rest of the monkeys. I didn't have time to close the gate. In a flash every one of them ran screaming and screeching out of the pen.

I ran for it. The monkeys came after me.

I was leading the pack. Banana Boy followed me and The Big Pee followed him. All the monkeys ran behind us.

It was a weird, wonderful feeling. I was the leader of the bunch. Banana Boy jumped up onto my shoulder. In the middle of all this panic I felt what it was like to be liked. My first friend was a dog. And my second one was a monkey.

Both in the same day. The world is a strange place.

The Big Pee screeched and snarled. He didn't like it. And he didn't like me anymore. I was a rival. He pushed Banana Boy from my shoulder with one sweep of his hand. Then he grabbed my foot and I fell.

The tribe swept along the path, leaving me sprawled on the ground. They swarmed up and over the fence of the zoo like a stream of giant ants. Only Banana Boy stayed perched on the top, looking down at me.

'Go,' I gasped. 'While you can.'

Banana Boy gave one timid blink and then he was gone.

I quickly jumped to my feet and ran out of the zoo before I got the blame for letting the monkeys out.

The monkeys were nowhere to be seen. I guessed they would be heading for the countryside. They would be safe in the bush. And free. That made me feel good.

But I was so tired. I could feel the call of my own bed even though it was only early afternoon. I wanted to fall asleep with big Bad Bear next to me. He was only a toy. But boy, was he big.

I hurried back into town listening carefully for the sound of motorbikes. I jumped every time I heard an engine. This whole thing was so weird. It couldn't be happening. I kept hoping that I would wake up.

But I didn't. The people passing by were real. They sniffed and screwed up their noses. I stank of fertiliser. I smelled of monkeys and elephants. People stared at me. What were they looking at?

I peered at a shop window and saw my reflection. My hair was all sticking to my head like a wet mop. I had the smelliest haircut in the world.

This was terrible. I tried to keep myself calm.

I started to think about what was happening to me. I was Chameleon Boy. My clothes and skin changed whenever I got scared.

No one would ever believe what had happened in the zoo. I could hardly believe it myself. It was good when I had Banana Boy as a friend. And Sandy. But now they were both gone. And I was all alone. A sad feeling settled on me like a cold fog.

Then I heard a sound.

'Ruff, ruff, ruff.'

'Sandy,' I yelled.

The fog melted away.

I was so pleased to
see Sandy that I hardly
noticed a van had
pulled up on the
other side of the road.
It had a wire cage in the back.

Sandy was happy too.

But not for long.

The van had the words
CITY POUND written on
the side. A man and a woman
stepped out. They each wore ranger badges.

Sandy ran over to greet them. He jumped up
and licked at one of them.

'Oh, no, Sandy, don't,' I yelled.

I was too late. In a flash they had a rope around
his neck. The two rangers lifted him into the cage
in the back of the van and slammed the gate closed.
They were taking him off to the pound.

'Give him back,' I begged. 'He's my dog.'

The woman smiled at me. 'Where's his collar?'
she said in a gentle voice. 'Where's his tag?'

I didn't know what to say.

'How long have you had him?' she said.

'All day,' I said.

She smiled again. 'He's not yours,' she said.

'What will happen to him?' I yelled.

'Someone might want him,' she said. 'He's not much to look at but you never know…'

'What if no one wants him?'

This time she didn't know what to say.

'I'm going to adopt him,' I said.

She gave me a little pat on the head. 'You're too young,' she said. 'But come back with your dad and he's yours.'

'I haven't got a dad,' I said.

My dad hadn't been around since I was three years old and I didn't know where he was. I used to wonder what his job was. Probably a pilot. Or a film star. Mum didn't like talking about him.

'Your mum then?' said the ranger.

'She won't have him,' I said. 'We can't afford a dog.'

The rangers looked at me sadly. Then they got into their van.

Sandy began to whimper. He peered out from

the other side of the cage with big, scared eyes. He didn't like it in there. He gave little squeals as the van moved off.

I started to run after the van. 'Sandy, Sandy,' I called.

The van went faster and faster.

'I will come and get you,' I yelled. 'I love you.'

I tried to keep up but it was no good. The van turned the corner and was gone.

I stopped running and tried to catch my breath. I had to do something. I had to talk Mum into adopting Sandy. But I knew she wouldn't. I couldn't stop thinking about it. What if no one wanted Sandy? What then?

I kept walking and worrying. Every now and then I checked my reflection in a shop window. To make sure that I still looked like me.

After a bit I found myself standing outside the Saturday market. There were stalls that sold just about anything you could think of. Rocking horses, clocks, chickens, toys and many other things.

There were a lot of people around. Parents, babies in prams. And even kids from my school. I made sure that none of them saw me. I didn't want to be noticed. Suddenly I saw horrible Gertag walking straight towards me.

I pressed myself back against a wall that had a great big map of the world hanging from it. I didn't want to be seen by Gertag. And hear her calling me What's His Name. I couldn't think of anything worse.

Yes I could.

'He's around here somewhere,' said a voice. 'I'm sure I saw him coming this way.'

It was Metal Mouth. I would know the sound of those clicking teeth anywhere. And Maggot. And The Chief and Shark. They were still after me. Oh, no, no, no, no, no.

I was filled with fear. I started to pant. I went cold. Then hot. It was like I was drowning. I couldn't get enough air.

'Please, not now,' I said to myself. 'Don't change. I have to get Sandy out of the lock-up.'

I stood there and stared at the four tough men.

They were looking for me. I was dead meat if they found me. They would never forgive me for touching their bikes. In the eyes of a bikie, it was the worst crime you could commit.

I stood there. But they didn't see me. Even though I was right in front of their noses.

I could hear what they were saying.

'Poor old Granny,' said The Chief. 'She bought me that bike. And now it's wrecked. What are we going to tell her?'

No wonder they were so mad. Their grandmother had bought them their motorbikes. And I had knocked them over and ruined them. Their Granny would be unhappy and miserable. All because of me.

'She doesn't laugh anymore,' said Shark.

'Not even a smile,' said Maggot.

'It's enough to make you cry,' said Metal Mouth.

'She looked after us for all those years,' said Maggot.

'Never complained once,' said Shark.

'Cooked all those meals,' said The Chief.

'And now she's so upset,' said Shark.

'Just sits there all day,' said Maggot.

'Unhappy.'

'Miserable.'

'We have to put things right.'

I tried to make sense of it. How come they all cared about the same old lady?

Then it struck me.

They were brothers.

The four top men in the bikie gang had the same grandmother.

Maggot had tears in his eyes. So did Shark. They all did. They were really worried about her. She was probably in an old folks' home. I could just picture her sitting there sadly in a wheelchair.

I started to feel a bit sorry for them. Even big bad bikies can have feelings. And I felt sorry for their poor old grandmother as well.

But if the brothers caught me I would be history. My legs began to tremble. How I wished that I had never touched one of their bikes.

That was when I noticed that Maggot was staring at me. With a strange look on his face.

'Hey, look,' he said. He pointed to me.

The brothers all screwed up their eyes and examined me.

'It's a person,' said Shark.

'A small kid,' said Metal Mouth.

'Painted all over like a map,' said The Chief.

It was true. I had blended with the map on the wall. My shirt, shorts, arms and legs were all covered in lines and rivers and countries. I could see Tasmania on my pants. And New Zealand off to one side.

'Is he real?' said Metal Mouth. He gave me a poke just below King Island.

'Ouch,' I yelped.

They all jumped back.

'It's one of those street acts,' said Maggot. 'All painted up.'

They all laughed.

'He's good,' said The Chief. 'Real good. You'd swear he was a statue.' He tossed fifty cents at my feet. Metal Mouth put down twenty cents and Shark gave a dollar.

'He's worth more than that,' said Maggot. 'Well done, kiddo,' he said to me. He put a five-dollar note down at my feet.

This was amazing. They thought I was a street act. They liked me. Perhaps they weren't so mean after all.

But I knew that they would soon change their tune if they knew who I was. The kid who had wrecked their bikes.

I stood still and tried not to blink.

Maggot got right up close. I seemed to make him a bit sad.

'This kid's face reminds me of something,' he said.

'Bali,' said Metal Mouth.

'Hong Kong,' said Shark.

'The Bungle Bungles,' said The Chief.

They walked away laughing. They thought I was funny.

All except Maggot. He followed them slowly, sometimes taking a look back at me.

'I know,' he said. 'He's got a face like the plant in the zoo.'

I stood there for ages. A living map. A lot of people stopped and peered at me. Some threw coins at my feet.

How long would this go on for? I knew I would stay blended in for as long as I was scared. As long as people looked at me.

After a bit the crowd thinned out. I started to feel safer.

Then, without warning, things began to change. The map of King Island sank into the sea and was followed quickly by Tasmania. Finally even the pictures of oceans and rivers drained from my body. I was just a boy with normal skin and clothes.

I walked quietly out of the market and into the street.

I had to stay calm. Take my thoughts away from peering eyes. Or danger. Think of nice things. Banana Boy, Sandy, Bad Bear. Mum.

But it didn't work for long. There on the side of the street was a line of motorbikes. Thirty black Harleys. And thirty big, bad bikies.

6.

The bikies were sitting on their damaged bikes with their helmets on. Ready to go. They hadn't seen me yet.

I was filled with fear. I started to pant. Oh, no. It was happening again. I went cold. Then hot. It was like I was drowning. I couldn't get enough air.

Bearded faces turned. Sunglasses flashed in my direction.

I could feel my body trying to change. I fought it. I tried to calm down. But the sound of their rough voices made me shake. The thought of what they would do to the boy who knocked over their bikes was too much.

Something changed. Something had happened

to me but I didn't know what it was. It was different to before. It was more than just blending.

'Look,' said Maggot. 'Look.'

They had found me. They could see me. Their eyes opened wide. Their mouths broke into smiles.

Smiles.

They started to laugh. Their big bellies shook. Tears rolled down their faces. The four brothers and the rest of the gang. They fell about wetting themselves.

What? What? What? What did they see?

'He looks a bit like Maggot,' said Metal Mouth.

'Yeah, a dork,' said The Chief.

What was so funny?

I examined myself. I was still me. A very small boy. But my own clothes had gone. My shoes. My pants. My jumper. All gone.

I had big leather boots. And jeans. And a bomber jacket with chains and studs.

My hands were covered in tattoos. Snakes and knives and a dragons. I had a silver skull on my collar.

I reached up and touched my face.

Whiskers.

I had a beard.

I was a bikie with all the equipment.

I touched my ear. An earring. Under my arm I held a small black motorbike helmet. I touched my head.

'Aargh.' I was bald.

I caught a glimpse of myself in a shop window. I was a tiny bikie. I even had a tattoo of a spider on my forehead. I shivered. I hated spiders.

'A shrimp,' said Metal Mouth.

'The smallest bikie in the world.'

The Chief and Shark laughed and laughed. Maggot didn't laugh. He was friendlier than the others. But more dangerous. He was trying to figure out who I was.

The Chief stopped laughing. 'Who are you? What do you want?' he said.

I couldn't think of an answer. I couldn't tell them I was the boy they were looking for. The one who had knocked over their motorbikes and damaged them.

'He's just a kid,' said Metal Mouth.

'Kids don't grow beards,' said The Chief.

'Could be a fake,' said Metal Mouth.

Shark reached over and gave my beard a tug.

'Ouch,' I shouted. 'That hurt.'

They all laughed again.

'Go easy,' said Maggot. 'He's only a little bloke.'

I had to do something. I had to make them forget about my real self.

I blurted out the first thing that came into my mind. Maybe it was something that had been inside me all along. Maybe I was born with the feeling. It was something I had never said before.

'I want to join the gang,' I whispered.

This time they really laughed. All except Maggot.

'Buzz off,' growled Metal Mouth. 'We have unfinished business. And it's not with you.'

'Yeah, get lost,' said Shark. 'Who do you think you are?'

It was a good question. Who was I? Just a little kid. What's His Name. That's who I was. A boy so nervous that he blended in like a lizard whenever he was in the spotlight. They weren't interested in a dork like me.

I turned and started to walk away slowly. I was getting away. And that was good.

But I was a nobody.

I had to face it. A dog in the pound. A monkey in a tree. And a giant-sized toy bear in a bed. These were my mates. I would never have a friend who was a boy. Or even human.

I was different to everyone else. There was no

one in the world like me. There never had been and there never would be.

Suddenly one of them spoke.

'Stop.'

It was Maggot.

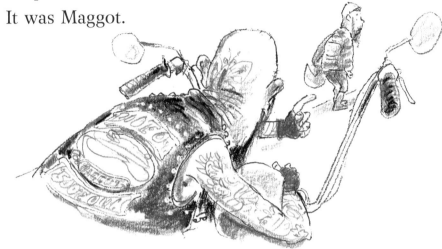

'Come back here, kiddo,' he said.

I turned and walked back with a sinking heart.

'He's just what we need,' Maggot said.

The other three looked puzzled.

'Why would we want a little squirt like him?' said Shark.

'I get it,' said The Chief.

'A mascot,' said Maggot. He smiled.

'The very thing,' said The Chief. 'A little mascot. The last one has gone. And won't be back.'

7.

For a moment the bikies all looked sad at the mention of their old mascot.

They muttered and mumbled among themselves. Then they started to nod and smile.

'Just the shot.'

'It's what we need.'

'Granny will love him.'

'Maybe she will. And maybe she won't,' said Metal Mouth.

The Chief held up a hand and all the other bikies looked his way. All twenty-nine of them. He pointed at me.

'Our new mascot,' he shouted. 'Yes or no.'

There was a silence. They were thinking. No one moved.

Then Maggot held out a closed fist with his

thumb pointing out to the side. They all did the same. Thirty clenched fists with thirty thumbs sticking out to the side like broken branches on dead trees.

Maggot slowly turned his thumb up, pointing at the sky. The Chief did the same. So did Shark. And finally Metal Mouth. And then, one by one, starting with the front bike, the gang members gave their response.

Yes, a turned-up thumb. And another and another. Finally, only one bikie was left to respond. He was busy looking at his own reflection in a shop window and stroking his red beard. He didn't know what was going on. He turned his thumb down.

'Loser,' said Maggot.

Red Beard looked sheepish and quickly turned up his thumb.

'Come with us,' Maggot said to me.

This was unbelievable. I was their mascot. The smallest bikie in the world. If they knew I was a boy they wouldn't have taken me. But the beard had fooled them. They thought I was a man.

I looked around. Maybe I could make a run for it. But I was surrounded. The four brothers walked to their battered bikes. Thirty motors exploded into life. Maggot pointed to the back seat of his Harley. I tried to throw a leg over but I couldn't. It was too tall for me and I fell to the ground.

Maggot gave a friendly laugh and put his hands under my arms. He picked me up and dumped me onto the seat. Then he mounted the bike and let out the clutch.

We were off. We swept down the road. Thunder on wheels. Thirty bikes. Thirty bikies. And me.

As we roared down the road people stopped and stared. Kids pointed. Cars pulled over to let us pass.

I was scared. I wanted to be home in my nice little bedroom. But here I was. One of the gang. I was the same but different. I belonged. I was their mascot, and that was good. But I was afraid.

They liked me. They wanted me. But for how long? I shuddered and scratched my beard. It was itchy.

I knew that once I relaxed I would lose my beard and all the other bits. Then they would see that I was the boy who bent their bikes. And I would be scared all over again.

There was something else to worry about, too. A poor dog with no ears. In the City Pound. Whimpering and sad. Unwanted and unloved. What if someone awful adopted him? Or no one? What then?

And what about the monkeys? I was worried about them. Where were they? How would they survive?

After about half an hour the bikie convoy turned into a wide driveway. There was a sign that read:

KOROIT CARAVAN PARK

That's when I realised what all this was about. The bikies expected me to cheer Granny up because she missed their old mascot. They thought I was funny. That's why they wanted me.

I started to tremble. What was I supposed to do? Stand on my head? Pull a funny face? I could just imagine her. A little old grey-haired lady – in a wheelchair, probably. Or bent over with a walking stick.

The bikies would be angry if I failed to amuse their grandmother. Could I make her laugh?

I didn't even have to try. I was funny as I was. A joke. Just a shrimp with a beard.

For some reason I didn't worry about them all looking at me. Maybe it was the beard. It was sort of like wearing a mask. They couldn't see the real me. But they would if I got too relaxed.

We swept through the caravan park. It was empty except for a few tents and a group of permanent rental vans up the back. There were a few chickens running around and T-shirts hanging off a line.

The bikies slowed and formed a big circle beside the vans.

That's when I saw her. Granny.

And her machine.

She was standing next to a huge black three-wheeler motorbike. A tough-looking lady with

tatts and earrings. And long black hair. She wore a leather bomber jacket with a drawing of a jet-powered three-wheeler with flames blasting out of the back.

She gave a smile as the thirty bikies killed their engines.

'My boys,' she said. 'My lovely boys.' All the bikies looked pleased. Especially her four grandsons.

She was big. But she didn't look bad. She had a kind face and a twinkle in her eye. Like Bad

Bear. He was big. But he wasn't bad. And his eyes twinkled, even though they were made of glass.

'Well, boys,' said Granny, 'what have you got for me?'

The smile fell from her lips. She seemed to be remembering something sad.

Maggot took his helmet off and stood by me proudly. The Chief grabbed me under the arms and lifted me out of the seat.

He dumped me on the grass.

'A new mascot,' he said.

A silence fell over the group. Thirty bikies waited to see what she thought. Would she like me? Would I cheer her up?

I started to shake.

She stared at my bald head and my tatts and my boy's face with a beard.

Seconds ticked by. If she liked me I was in trouble because I would feel safe. Then I would turn back into a boy. And they would recognise me. Then I would be scared all over again and blend in with something else. I couldn't win whichever way it went.

But in my heart I wanted her to like me. If she turned her thumb down I would be chased off. Or worse.

I looked up at her. Pleading with my eyes.

Finally she spoke.

'He's lovely,' she said. 'But shouldn't he be in school?'

'With a beard?' said The Chief.

She looked at me without speaking for ages. Then she held out a fist with a thumb sticking out to the side. And gave me the thumbs-up, followed by a smile.

I was in. But my mind was swirling. There was another person to think about. Mum. I had to go back to her. She didn't have anyone else.

I had to do something. Or say something, at least.

'Where's your old mascot?' I said in a squeaky, trembling voice.

'Fearless ran off,' said The Chief. 'And we can't find him.'

I could see Fearless in my mind. A giant warrior. Scared of nothing. He probably rode a thumping big Harley that could thrash the pants off every bike on the road. And the new mascot was just a shy kid with a beard.

I saw tears forming in Granny's eyes.

'Dear Fearless,' she said. 'His hearing wasn't too good. But he was a great mascot.'

Dear Fearless? Her words started to stir up thoughts. Fearless. Fearless. What did that remind me of?

Fearless, Fearless, think, think.

Yes, yes, yes.

Fearless.

Earless.

Sandy, the dog with no ears.

Fearless was their missing mascot. The bikies hadn't been chasing me at all. It wasn't me they were looking for. They were just chasing after their lost dog. Not the boy who bumped their bikes.

I had got it all wrong. Made a mistake.

I looked at thirty pairs of eyes staring at their new mascot.

I wasn't as scared as before. But I was still worried. A bent bike is not something a bikie forgets too easily. I had to get out of this mess.

'I know where Fearless is,' I said.

There was a long silence.

'Are you joking?' said The Chief.

I shook my head.

'Prove it,' clicked Metal Mouth.

'He is a sandy colour,' I said. 'No ears. And one eye is blue and the other brown.'

Granny's eyes filled with tears. 'It's him,' she said. 'Fearless is alive.'

'Take us there. Now,' growled Shark.

My brain changed up a gear. I was really rolling.

'If I take you to Fearless, will you forgive me?' I said.

'For what?' said The Chief.

'For anything,' I said.

Granny took a step towards me. 'If you find my dog,' she said, 'the world is yours. All is forgiven. Whatever it is.'

They all smiled and nodded their heads.

They weren't big bad bikies at all. They were just people who liked motorbikes. I felt good. And I felt relaxed.

A warm feeling started to flow through my body. No one had noticed, but my bikie boots had gone. In their place were my own shoes.

My tattoos began to fade. I could feel myself changing.

I couldn't let them see what was happening.

Their minds would be blown if they saw a bearded bikie change into a small boy. Who knew what would happen with so many people making a fuss over me? I might grow feathers like one of the chooks. Or worse. I quickly ducked down behind Maggot's bike.

In a flash, my bomber jacket disappeared. The hair was back on my head. My beard went away. I was my old self. Just like everyone else. No – the same, but different. And it felt great.

I jumped out from behind the bike and held up my arms.

'Ta da,' I said.

The bikies all gasped. They were impressed. But not shocked.

'How did he do that?' said Metal Mouth.

'What a trick,' said The Chief.

'He's a little magician,' said Metal Mouth.

'I knew the beard was a fake,' said Shark.

'It's him,' said Metal Mouth. 'The kid who bumped our bikes.'

They all shook their heads. Some of them looked cross. But a promise was a promise. No one complained. And anyway, I had made Granny happy.

Maggot looked at me with a funny expression. Then he grinned and lifted me up onto the back of his bike and started the engine. Thirty-one bikes roared at the sky.

I pointed to the gate.

'Let's go,' I shouted.

Granny led the way on her three-wheeler. She was the real boss of the gang. We roared through the streets. It felt good sitting there behind Maggot with my arms around his waist.

Finally we pulled up at the pound.

The gang crowded into the office. Through a window I could see cats in pens. But no dogs. A ranger came into the office and looked startled to see so many people in the room.

It was the woman who had put Sandy in the van. Maggot banged a fifty-dollar note down on the counter in front of her.

'What's that for?' said the ranger.

'The dog with no ears,' he said. 'It's ours.'

'It's got no tag,' said the ranger.

Granny took over. She held up a broken collar covered in metal studs.

'This is his,' she growled.

The ranger read the tag and nodded.

'Wait here,' she said.

In no time at all the ranger was back with Sandy. Or should I say Fearless. He wagged his tail happily. The bikies nodded and grinned. I could see that they all loved him. The ranger handed Fearless over to Maggot and all the bikies started to pat the happy dog.

Sandy began to bark with excitement. He looked at me. He looked at Granny. He didn't know who to run to first. Sandy liked us both.

I held out my hands and squatted down. 'Sandy,' I yelled. 'Come to me.'

Granny held out her hands and squatted down. 'Fearless,' she growled. 'Come to me.'

He looked at me. He looked at her.

'Sandy,' I yelled.

'Fearless,' said Granny.

Sandy didn't know what to do. But in the end he did the right thing. He scampered to Granny and jumped all over her. She was so happy.

After a bit he came and licked my hand.

Granny nodded. 'That kid's all right,' she said. 'From now on he's one of us.'

'If his mum says it's okay,' said Maggot.

On the way out Granny winked at me and held out a closed fist. She opened it and showed me something. It was a dog biscuit.

I wanted to say something funny. Because she cheated. But I was too shy. So I just gave a little smile.

She winked at me again and then tapped her nose.

The gang dropped me off near home. Maggot handed me a piece of paper.

'What's this?' I said.

'My phone number,' he said. 'Give it to your mum.'

As I walked through the park I thought about my life. I felt much happier than I had that morning. The bikies were my new friends. Especially Maggot. But only if Mum agreed.

And Sandy was my dog. Sort of.

But I was still shy. And I had to find a way to

stop blending in. I had to get control of myself.

I made my way through the trees and headed to the place where the whole thing had started. The place where the two little statues stood by the road. But when I got there I found that things had changed.

Only one lonely stone boy stood there squirting water out of his mouth. The other one had gone.

Someone must have stolen it.

I stared at the one that was left. Somehow I kept feeling that the missing statue had seemed just a little bit different. Like with identical twins; when you get to know them you can tell which is which.

'Where's your mate gone?' I said.

I wished he was alive. I wished he was my friend. But he was made of rock.

And didn't say a thing.

It would be good to get home. I decided not to tell Mum about my problems. About blending in and all that. She wouldn't believe me. Who would? And she would start to worry. And want to take me to see a doctor. And the doctor wouldn't believe it either. And then what?

I was looking forward to my own room. And my own bed. To peace and quiet. And to falling asleep with Bad Bear. I was so tired from my big day. And it wasn't over yet. Not by a long way.

I went through the back door and into the kitchen. I heard voices. It was Mum and…

Oh, no. My heart turned to ice. I had forgotten. Gertag was staying with us. And she was already there.

9.

I crept upstairs to my room. I started to hide everything. My books, my Transformers, my skateboard. I had to be quick. Before Gertag got up to her usual tricks.

I picked up Bad Bear and looked around. There was nowhere to hide him. He was as big as me. His eyes seemed to see, even though they were made of glass. His mouth was pulled back into a snarl. It wasn't his fault that he looked weird. I had dropped him on his head once when I was little. And a car ran over him. His teeth got mashed up when he hit the road. But I still loved him.

And Gertag knew that I did. I heard her footsteps coming.

I jumped behind the curtains. Bad Bear was still on the bed.

The door crashed open.

'He's not here,' said Gertag.

'Where has that boy gone?' said Mum.

I stayed in my hiding place. And kept quiet.

'Can I have Bad Bear, please?' said Gertag. Her voice was like honey.

'No, dear,' said Mum. 'Bad Bear is special.'

I heard Gertag stamp on the floor. Then the door closed. I was alone. But I knew that I would have to go and be nice to her sooner or later.

I could hear Mum calling.

'Dinnertime. Come down and have your dinner.'

I stayed where I was. No way was I going to sit down there and be nice to Gertag. Okay, I was hungry. But I had emergency supplies.

Burp Bombs. I could make a Burp Bomb last for two hours if I sucked slowly. I was looking forward to a good slurp. Burp Bombs were delicious.

I pulled open the top drawer of my bedside table. There was only one Burp Bomb left. Someone must have pinched the other one.

Mum sent Gertag upstairs to call me for tea. I could hear her opening doors. I listened to her calling out softly so that Mum couldn't hear what she was saying.

'Where are you, little What's His Name?'

I didn't answer. She gave up and went down-stairs.

I had to go. I knew that. So I followed her down. Mum was dishing up stir-fry. Oh, no. Not Mum's stir-fry again.

It always had something new in it that she had discovered. Mongolian devil grass. Or dried crickets. Or furry nuts. And other stuff that tasted like sawdust.

I thought she might have made something else for our visitor. But it probably wouldn't have made any difference because everything Mum made tasted the same. I never told her that, of course. I just said, 'Yum,' and swallowed quickly.

'What's that smell?' said Mum.

I couldn't tell her that it was monkey mixed with elephant and a bit of dog sweat on the side. So I changed the subject. Gertag was sucking something.

'She ate my Burp Bomb,' I said softly.

Gertag smiled with her mouth. But her eyes did not smile.

'He had two,' she said. She got up and went upstairs so that she didn't have to answer any questions.

Mum looked at me. 'You have to share,' she said. 'You have to give your visitor half. You know that.'

'She didn't even ask,' I said.

I forced down Mum's stir-fry and went upstairs to have a shower. Then I put on my pyjamas and got into bed with Bad Bear. I was glad that no one at school knew about him. They would all laugh if someone told them I had a toy bear.

I could never get to sleep
without Bad Bear. I put my
arms around him and tipped
him over. He gave a soft growl.
For some reason Bad Bear's
growl made me feel safe. Even
though he was only a stuffed
toy with a battery inside him.

I decided to cheer myself up by eating the last Burp Bomb. I opened the drawer. Gertag had been in my room again. There was only half of the last Burp Bomb left. Why did she have to spoil everything? I quickly ate it, then fell asleep thinking about my weird, weird day.

And not knowing that the next one would be even weirder.

THE SECOND DAY

10.

It was early in the morning. Still dark. Around one o'clock, I think. I was having a dream about the statue I had seen in the park. The one I thought had blinked its eyes at me. The one that had disappeared.

Right in the middle of the dream a noise woke me up. I opened my eyes but couldn't see a thing. There was a scratching at the window. Someone was outside.

It couldn't be Gertag. There was no way she could climb up to the first-floor window.

I stared out into the black night. Then I made it out: a face at the window.

I wanted to turn on the light but I couldn't take my eyes off the face.

Finally I managed to stretch out my hand.

Click. The room was full of light. But now I couldn't see out the window properly. I could only make out two eyes. The eyes were looking, looking, looking.

I grabbed Bad Bear and hugged him. The face outside stared in.

I started to pant. I went cold. Then hot. It was like I was drowning. I couldn't get enough air. Oh, no. It was happening again. I was scared and I was changing.

I looked at my hands. Oh, what?

Oh, no, no, no, no, no.

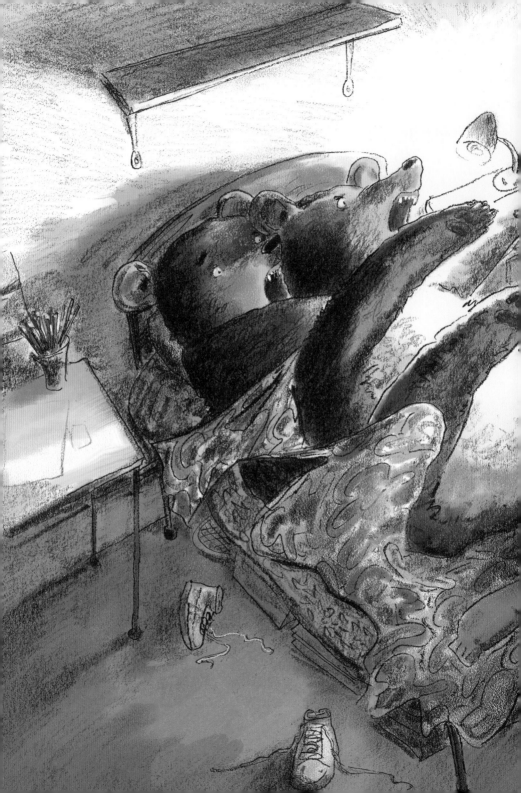

I was covered in fur. Brown fur.

Right at that moment I heard a knock.

The face at the window disappeared.

The door swung open.

It was Gertag. The noise must have woken her. She stared at me. Then at Bad Bear.

'Two,' she said to herself. 'That sneaky little What's His Name has got two bears.'

Oh, no. I was a copy of Bad Bear. I could see myself in the mirror.

But this was different to anything that had happened before. I wasn't just blending in. I wasn't just covered in fur. I was a *real* bear. With a snarl. And smashed teeth.

'What's His Name has to share,' Gertag said. She grabbed one of my paws and pulled.

Bump. I fell onto the floor.

'You're heavy,' she said.

Gertag started to drag me through the door and along the corridor. I was frozen with fear. I couldn't even move.

'Please, no, no, no,' I thought.

But it was no good. She pulled me into the spare bedroom and slammed the door.

Gertag tried to heave me up into the bed. But I was too heavy. I wasn't stuffed with straw like Bad Bear. I had guts and gizzards and a heart. The real Bad Bear didn't weigh much. I was heavy.

Gertag dropped me onto the floor. Then she shoved a pillow under my head. She smiled her terrible smile as she looked at my furry face. She covered me with her doona and snuggled in with me.

Oh, it was terrible. Oh, it was horrible. But there was worse to come.

'You're ugly,' said Gertag. 'But I like you.'

She put her lips up to mine.

Oh, what, what, what? She was kissing me. Her lips were all wet and sloppy and tasted of Burp Bomb.

I pushed her away with my paws and bounded to the door.

Gertag screamed.

I tried to twist the doorhandle with my claws but it was slippery. I backed into a corner and tried to wipe Gertag's spit off my lips.

A terrible growl came out of my mouth. The sound of it filled the room.

I was so scared.

But not as scared as Gertag.

She gave another huge scream and bolted out of the room. She ran down the corridor yelling and shouting.

'A bear, a bear, a bear. A real bear.'

11.

I lumbered back to my room on all fours. I was in a terrible state. I tried to call out, but all I could do was growl. I had to calm myself. I knew that relaxing was the only way to get back to normal. I would never be a boy again until I calmed down.

I glanced up at the window. The face was back. Looking in. Staring. Filling me with fear. There was no way I could relax.

I could hear Gertag shouting for Mum. And footsteps on the stairs. I had to hide. Mum wouldn't know it was me. She might attack me. And I wouldn't be able to fight back. I couldn't bite my own mother.

I quickly bunched up the covers with my paws to make it look like I was sleeping. Then I wiggled underneath the bed. I tried to stop panting.

I saw feet come into my room.

'It was just a bad dream,' Mum whispered to Gertag. 'Bad Bear is just a toy.'

She must have been looking at the toy Bad Bear. The springs squeaked above me as she sat down and picked him up.

'Bad Bear growls when you tip him,' said Mum. I heard Bad Bear's quiet growl.

'He was real,' yelled Gertag.

'Did you ask if you could have Big Bear?' Mum said in a quiet voice. She thought I was asleep under the covers.

'There were two of them,' said Gertag. 'I was sharing with What's...'

Mum's voice changed. She was annoyed.

'No, dear,' said Mum. 'There is only one Bad Bear. Not two. It was a birthday present his father gave him when he was a little boy. He can't get to sleep without Bad Bear.'

Gertag stamped her feet.

'There were two, there were two, there were two,' she shouted. 'And one ran away.'

There was a silence. I knew that Mum was

shaking her head. And looking at Gertag in the way that parents do when they don't believe you.

Gertag was angry but she said something wonderful.

'I want to go home.'

At first Mum didn't say anything. She wanted me to have a friend. Any friend. Even Gertag. I could almost see her thinking.

'Okay, Gertag,' said Mum with a sigh. 'If that's really what you want.'

They disappeared downstairs and I heard Mum talking to Gertag's mother on the phone. Not long after that, I heard a car horn toot and then the front door open. Mum had taken the terrible girl out to meet her mother.

It was such a relief.

Gertag was gone.

I stayed under the bed trying to stop panting. I tried to relax. I tried to calm down so that I would turn back into a boy. But it was no use. I was still a bear.

I couldn't stop thinking about the window. And the eyes staring in from the darkness.

I didn't want to look. But if you don't look you don't know. And then the fear is worse.

Then I realised something. If the person at the window saw me they wouldn't see a boy. They would see a bear. A walking, growling bear.

They would probably get a fright and run away.

I crawled out from under the bed and looked at the window.

The face outside pressed its nose to the glass. A dark, flat nose. Beady black eyes peered in.

Suddenly it gave a squeak. And then a squeal. Oh, no. Oh, yes. Yes, yes, yes. It wasn't a man. It wasn't a woman. It wasn't even a person.

It was a monkey.

The face at the window belonged to Banana Boy.

Slowly, slowly, slowly, the fur on my arms began to thin out. My paws began to grow fingers. And my feet began to grow toes. I was like a plant beginning to shoot and grow buds.

In no time at all I was my normal self again. Legs, arms, fingers, belly button. It was all there.

'What are you doing here, Banana Boy?' I yelled through the window. 'Is it just you? Where are all the other monkeys? How did you find me?'

He couldn't answer. He was a monkey. He just sat there on the windowsill, shivering. Then he held out a tiny hand. I could see that he was frightened. And probably hungry.

At that moment Mum rushed through the door.

'What's going on?' she said. 'What's happening now? What are you yelling at? What did you see?'

'A monkey,' I said. 'From the zoo. Look.'

Mum peered into the black night. There was nothing there.

'It must have been a possum,' she said. She gave a little laugh.

'No, it was a monkey,' I said. 'I saw him at the zoo today. His name is Banana Boy.'

Mum looked at me strangely. 'Well,' she said. 'If you say so, dear.'

She patted me on the head and led me back to bed.

I decided to tell Mum the whole thing after all. That's what mothers are for. And fathers.

'I was a bear,' I said.

'What?' said Mum.

'Whenever people stare at me,' I said, 'I get nervous. And then I blend in like a chameleon. At first it was just blending in. Like bark on a tree. And then I started changing. I grew a beard like a bikie's.'

Mum's look changed. She thought I was up to something.

'You grew a beard? I don't think so.'

'I did,' I said. 'But now it's worse. I actually turned into a bear. I was a copy. A real copy of Bad Bear.'

'You didn't frighten Gertag with Bad Bear, did you?' said Mum. 'You didn't pretend that Bad Bear was real?'

She was beginning to get cross. She thought I had scared Gertag on purpose.

I could see that she didn't believe me but I kept going. It was time she knew about my problem. I needed help.

'You know I get shy. At school I don't speak. I just listen. I don't like it when people look at me. I don't like it when teachers ask me questions. Gertag knows what I'm like. She calls me What's His Name.'

'She shouldn't do that,' said Mum. 'But you don't really change. You just…'

She was searching for words to describe it.

'...blend in,' she said.

'Yes,' I shouted.

'Not like a chameleon,' she said quickly. 'Not like that. You sort of shrink down. You don't meet people's eyes. You are just very, very shy.'

I met her eyes. I didn't even blink.

'I was a bear,' I said.

Mum shook her head and tried not to look cross.

'Show me,' she said. 'Do it now. Go on. Copy something.'

'I can't,' I said. 'I can't *make* it happen. I only change when I'm scared.'

'Boo,' said Mum in a loud voice.

'That's no good,' I said. 'I'm not scared of *you*. But if other people look at me I start to get hot and cold and shiver and then I blend in and they can't see me.'

I started to cry. 'I hate it,' I sobbed. 'I just want to be normal. Like everyone else.'

Mum stroked my forehead. And gave me a cuddle.

'We will get help for you,' she said. 'The doctor. Or school counsellor. They will explain it to you. They will help you understand that you were not a bear. It was just a nightmare. Go to sleep. I'll sit here until you do.'

It was no use. She would never believe me. I snuggled under the doona. Mum turned down the light and held my hand.

12.

I tried to fall asleep but I had never felt more alone. Even with Mum there holding my hand. I was too worried about what was happening to me. And I couldn't stop thinking about Banana Boy and the other monkeys that had escaped from the zoo. They would be hungry and cold. I had to find them. I had to do something. But I needed help.

'I wish I had a dad,' I said to Mum.

'You do have a dad,' she said. 'You know that.'

'I can't even remember him,' I said.

'He remembers you,' said Mum.

I looked at the photo of him holding me when I was only three.

He was standing in the backyard of our old house. The place where we lived before he left me

and Mum. He was handsome.
He had thick black hair and
was wearing bathers. He
had me in one arm and
a cat in the other.

'Where is he?' I said.

'I'm not quite sure,'
said Mum. 'He's gone up north somewhere.'

'Why can't I see him?' I said. 'Where is he?
Why doesn't he ring us?'

'I've told you a hundred times,' said Mum.
'He had a problem. An illness. He was terrified
of spiders. He thinks it stops him being a good
father. He said he will come and see you if he ever
gets over it.'

'Everyone's scared of spiders,' I said.

'Not like him,' said Mum. 'There's a bit I haven't
told you. Something bad happened.'

'What was it?' I said, but Mum was quiet. 'Tell
me,' I said.

Mum sighed. Then she started to talk. Her
voice was soft, like the radio turned down low.
She gave my hand a little squeeze.

'You were only three,' said Mum. 'So you won't remember what happened. Your dad took you to the park to feed the ducks. A spider ran up his leg. Inside his jeans.'

'What happened?' I said to Mum.

'He started jumping around and yelling,' said Mum. 'He was terrified. He tore off his pants and shirt and started whacking at his back trying to get rid of the spider.'

'Then what?' I said.

'You got scared and backed away. You fell into the lake. You were drowning but he didn't see you. He was too busy trying to get rid of the spider. A girl jumped in and saved you.'

'What girl?'

'A teenager, from the high school. Her photo was in the local paper. She was a hero.'

'What about Dad?' I said. 'Was he in the paper too?'

'Yes,' said Mum. 'He was ashamed. He felt like a coward every time he looked at you.'

'It was my fault,' I said.

'No, it wasn't,' said Mum. 'It wasn't anyone's fault.'

I put my hand up and touched her face. It was wet.

'Is he dead?' I said.

'No, don't be silly,' said Mum. 'He sends me money. And I send him pictures of you.'

'I want him back,' I said.

'So do I,' said Mum. 'He said he will come back when he is better.'

She had a faraway look in her eyes. I tried to cheer her up by changing the subject.

'I've got a new friend,' I said.

'A new friend,' said Mum. 'Who?'

'A bloke with a motorbike,' I said.

'A man?' Mum did not sound pleased. 'Who is he? How do you know him?'

'He's in a bikie gang,' I said. 'They're new in town. They're all really friendly. I knocked over their bikes and they let me off.'

Mum went quiet for a few seconds. I couldn't tell what she was thinking. Was it 'yes' or was it 'no'? 'What does this man look like?' said Mum.

I couldn't tell her the truth. If I said that he was bald and had tattoos and earrings and a bushy beard she wouldn't like it. So I lied.

'He has neat hair and wears a suit,' I said. 'He's a doctor. A brain surgeon.'

'A bikie wearing a suit,' said Mum. 'Don't give me that.'

'He is a really great guy,' I said.

'He might be a good bloke,' said Mum, 'but…' She let the words die. She didn't seem to know what to say. But I knew what she was thinking.

'He is too old to be your friend,' she said. 'You don't know who he is. You can't go around with a man.'

'Why not?' I said. 'If I can't have a dad, I can have a man friend, can't I? It'd be good for me.'

I handed a piece of paper to Mum.

'What's this?' she said.

'His phone number. He told me to give it to you.'

'Maggot,' she shouted. 'A brain surgeon called Maggot?'

Mum looked at me wildly. She was in shock.

'I will be talking to Mr Maggot,' she said. 'That's one thing for sure. You need a friend but his name isn't Maggot.'

'Or Gertag,' I said.

'Go to sleep,' said Mum. 'I'm turning off the light now.' She sat there for a while and then crept out of the room and quietly closed the door.

I finally drifted off to sleep with thoughts of monkeys and spiders running around in my head.

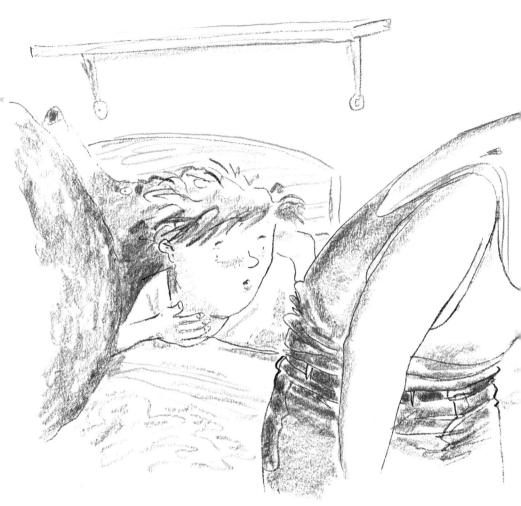

In the morning Mum had some news.

'You were right,' she said excitedly. 'The monkeys from the zoo are in the news. They've all escaped and people are seeing them everywhere. You really did see a monkey.'

'I told you that,' I yelled. 'I know him. Banana Boy.'

Mum looked at me sadly. 'That bit was a dream,' she said.

I sighed. 'Well, I'm glad the monkeys are not in the zoo. They can live in the trees with the koalas. They can go where they like. They can eat whatever they like.'

'I wouldn't be so sure about that,' said Mum. 'I don't think they eat gumleaves.'

'They like bananas,' I said.

'Bananas don't grow in Victoria,' said Mum. 'It's too cold.'

'They'll be hungry,' I said. 'Really hungry.'

She nodded.

I wondered how Banana Boy had arrived at my window. He must have followed his nose. He knew my scent from the zoo.

'I'm going out,' I said. 'I have to find Banana Boy.'

'Not yet,' said Mum. 'You wait here until I go and check a few things out. Do the dishes and clean up your room. And stay home.'

'Aw, Mum,' I said.

She gave me one of those looks.

I knew not to argue. So I bit my tongue as she left the house. She was gone for ages. I did everything she said but I kept going out to the front gate and looking for her. I had to find those monkeys.

While I was waiting I filled up a bottle of water and grabbed a banana. I shoved them into my backpack. I was just about to nick off when Mum finally appeared at the end of the street.

I yelled out, 'Can I go now?'

She waved. Was that a 'yes' or was it a 'no'?

This time I didn't wait to find out. I grabbed my pack and ran for it. I thought she called out but I pretended not to hear. I had to find Banana Boy. Before he died of hunger.

13.

I walked down the street, keeping my eyes peeled. I looked up into the trees and on the rooftops but there was no sign of the monkeys.

Other people were also looking for the monkeys. Keepers from the zoo searched parks and riverbanks. I saw two policemen checking out a drain and gardeners scanning the tops of trees in the park. It was busy for a Sunday.

I really wanted to help the monkeys. But a dreadful thought kept creeping into my mind. I had turned into a copy of Bad Bear when I became nervous. Would I have this forever? Was I doomed to be different? Or would I grow out of it? I didn't want to be noticed but I didn't want to turn into something else either, that was for sure.

In front of me I saw two people from a TV station. A man and a woman were stopping people in the street and talking to them. The woman held a microphone. The man pointed his camera at me.

Oh, no. It was bad enough just being noticed. But to be seen on television would be the worst thing in the world. I quickly ducked behind a letterbox.

I started to pant. I went cold. Then hot. It was like I was drowning. I couldn't get enough air. Not again. I was changing. It was happening again.

'Where did that boy go?' said the guy with the camera.

The cameraman was looking straight at me. But he couldn't see me. Because there were two letterboxes by the side of the road.

And one of them was me.

I couldn't believe it. I had turned into a copy of the letterbox. Oh, this was terrible.

I couldn't see my own face but I knew that I still somehow had eyes and a mouth. I could see and I could breathe.

An old lady approached. Oh, no, no, no. She was holding a bunch of letters. She walked towards me. Then she lifted up my mouth flap and started to stuff a letter into it.

'Argh.' It hurt. All smooth and sharp.

The old lady became angry.

'It's blocked,' she said. 'Nothing works these days. The country is going to the dogs.'

She pulled the letter out of my mouth slot. Then she shoved it into the letterbox standing next to me. The real one.

'Where did that kid go?' said the cameraman.

The old lady pointed at me. 'There's something

stuck in there,' she said. 'It might be a monkey.'
She gave a little snort.

'A monkey couldn't get through the flap,' said
the cameraman.

He walked over towards me. I was nothing
more than a red box with a slot for a mouth. He
pushed my mouth flap open and stared in. It was
like being at the dentist's.

'Pooh,' he said to his friend. 'That letterbox has got bad breath.'

I could hear them laughing as they walked away down the street.

The old lady left, and I was still frozen to the footpath.

Life was not good.

It was driving me crazy. I couldn't just stay there all day like that. Waiting for the copy effect to go away.

'Think. Think, think, think.'

I had to relax. I had to get rid of the fear. I had to be able to let people stare at me. And not care about it.

'Relax, relax, relax,' I said inside my head. 'Relax, relax, relax.'

After a bit I could feel something happening. Yes, yes, yes. A warm feeling swept through my hard steel body. My arms came back. And my hands. Soon I was me again.

My time as a letterbox was over. I had all my bits. Just to be on the safe side I looked inside my pants. Yes, everything was there.

Relaxing had done the trick. It definitely seemed to be the secret. If I could relax, I could beat my fear.

I walked on, thinking about my father and keeping an eye out for the monkeys.

I stopped at a public toilet. I decided to go and see if any monkeys were hiding in there. But then I had a nasty thought.

What if I went into the toilet and something gave me a fright? I might turn into a copy of something. A hand basin. Or a toilet bowl.

What if I was a toilet bowl and someone walked in and sat…? No, no, no. I couldn't bear to even think about it. Horrible, horrible, horrible.

I pushed the thought out of my mind and kept going down the street. At that moment I heard a sound. A welcome sound. Motorbikes.

It was Granny and Shark and The Chief and Metal Mouth. And Maggot.

They pulled up with squealing brakes and killed their engines.

'It's our mascot,' yelled Maggot. He held up his hand and gave me a high five.

Granny sat on her three-wheeler like a queen. Sandy was perched on the back.

Maggot gave me a big smile.

'Hey, mate,' he said. 'What's new?'

I couldn't look him in the eyes. 'Mum won't let me see you,' I said.

There was a long silence.

'She says you're too old. And she doesn't like maggots.' The last bit was a lie. I was just trying to make him feel better.

That's when I noticed that they were all grinning.

'She has already paid us a visit,' said Granny. 'This morning.'

'And I'm invited over for tea,' said Maggot.

I couldn't believe it. They were all nodding. Was it true?

'She's cooking her special stir-fry.'

I sort of groaned and whooped at the same time. Mum had really invited him for tea. It was great news. She must have been feeling really sorry for me. Because I had no friends. Maybe she heard Gertag calling me What's His Name.

But Mum's stir-fry? Poor Maggot.

'What are you up to now?' said The Chief.

'I'm looking for the monkeys,' I said. 'They're my friends. And they're hungry.'

They didn't seem to know what to say.

'Better leave it to the experts,' said Metal Mouth. 'Monkeys have sharp teeth.'

I had to get them on side.

'We have to get them to a safe place,' I said. 'Into the bush. If the rangers come they will try to take them back to the zoo.'

Maggot clapped a hand on my shoulder. He looked at me seriously.

'What's it like for them at the zoo?' he said slowly. 'Their pen. What's it like?'

I knew the answer to that. So did he. 'It's really big, with trees and nets to climb and stuff like that.'

'What's the food like?'

'Good, plenty of bananas,' I said.

'What if they get sick?'

'They have vets,' I said.

'There are not many of those monkeys left in the wild,' said Maggot.

'Can't they go back?' I said.

He shook his head.

'Where they came from the forests have all gone,' he said. 'One day, maybe. When the trees have grown again.'

'We have forests,' I said.

'Wrong trees,' he said. 'There's nothing they can eat.'

We stared at each other.

I spoke slowly. 'They have to go back to the zoo, don't they?'

'They do, mate,' said Maggot. 'They do.'

'But they're scared,' I yelled. 'The monkeys might scatter. And get lost. And never find each other again. They will just run away. They don't like all the noise. They might get hurt. You have to help me get them back to the zoo. Now.'

Maggot looked at me with a kind grin. 'How could I do that, mate? We don't even know where they are.'

I pulled out the banana I had in my backpack.

'That won't go far,' said Metal Mouth.

'I know,' I said. 'But I'm going to Franky's Fruit Stall to buy some more.'

I put my hand in my pocket and felt the coins I had in there from yesterday, when people thought I was a busker. I held them out.

Maggot smiled and then nodded knowingly to the others. 'We have to go,' he said. 'Stay cool, man.'

The five of them started their engines and disappeared in a cloud of smoke and noise.

'You stay cool too,' I yelled.

14.

I walked on down the street, still looking for the monkeys. There was no sign of them, so I headed out into the countryside.

It took me ages to get to Franky's Fruit Stall. It was way out of town.

My heart sank when I finally got there. There was a sign on the window.

CLOSED. BACK LATER.

Rats. I stared through the window. There were plenty of bananas. But the place was locked up.

That's when I noticed it. Monkey poo. All over the place. The monkeys had been there but they couldn't get in.

A trail of poo ran down the road. Monkeys drop poo when they are frightened so there was plenty for me to follow.

The trail went for about a kilometre along the road and then turned off onto an old railway line that ran through the forest.

I could see that the poo was starting to dry out. I had to hurry.

The railway line wound further and further
into the forest. After about half an hour I reached
the end of the monkey poo trail. It stopped at a
ramshackle old building. An abandoned railway
station.

Grey, buckled planks clung desperately to the walls. The rusted tin roof was bent and filled with holes. Some of the windows were broken and the rest were covered in cobwebs. All the doors were gone.

I peered in. Everything was quiet. And dark.
'It's me,' I whispered. 'Don't be afraid, I've come
to help you.'

I heard a squeaking noise. The squeaking
turned to squealing. And then to hissing and
spitting. The monkeys were scared of me. They
seemed to have forgotten who I was.

A big monkey appeared at the door with arms swinging. His teeth were bared. It was the boss monkey – The Big Pee. He didn't remember me either – or maybe he did. I backed away. He was a powerful creature.

I took a step back towards the doorway. Before I could get any closer a small shape appeared out of the gloom. It was Banana Boy. He recognised me and stepped out onto the tracks.

'Hello, little fellow,' I said. 'I am here to help you.'

He looked tired and weak.

I reached into my backpack and took out the banana. I held it out to him.

He took one step forward. Then another. He reached out one trembling hand. He took the banana and started to peel it.

Suddenly The Big Pee grabbed the banana and swallowed it greedily. Then he disappeared back into the station, followed by Banana Boy.

I decided to go inside and talk to them. I tiptoed in. It was dark and at first I couldn't see anything. Then little pinpricks of light began to twinkle like distant stars above my head. Eyes. A hundred eyes were blinking at me from above.

Slowly my eyes adjusted to the light. The monkeys were all sitting in the rafters, looking down.

'Come on,' I said. 'You have to get out of here. Follow me.'

There was more nervous chattering. They were not going to budge.

Right then I saw it. Falling slowly like a leaf dropping from a tree. Before I could move, it settled on my arm.

'Aargh,' I shrieked.

A huge huntsman spider scampered over my hand.

I started to pant. I went cold. Then hot. It was like I was drowning. I couldn't get enough air.

Everything changed. The world appeared strange. I could see both sides of me without turning my head. I could see back, front and above. What was going on? What, what, what?

The monkeys were screeching in terror from their perch in the rafters.

Then I realised.

I had changed.

I had long black hairy legs. Eight of them.

I was a copy.

Of the spider.

Oh, please, please, get me back to normal. Help. Anyone. Please.

I was a spider as big as a goat. The monkeys were squealing and yelping above. Some ran out onto the railway line.

I walked around on my eight hairy legs. I could move quite quickly.

Everything seemed unreal. The world was crazy.

I started to do what spiders do after they fall.

I began to climb up the wall. I stopped at a high window. There were a lot of dead blowflies on the windowsill. They were all on their backs with their legs pointing up to the ceiling. A couple were still buzzing.

I didn't want to do it. But I was part boy and part spider. I just couldn't help it. My inner spider got the better of me.

I grabbed a dead fly with my front pincers and shoved it into my mouth. Then another, and another. I couldn't help myself. The flies were

crunchy. Like potato chips. Quite tasty actually. Not as good as Burp Bombs. But not bad.

I crawled up to the rafters. And then went a little higher. I reached the ceiling and began to move across it. Upside down.

Now I was looking down on the monkeys. They were terrified. The noise was incredible. They sounded like the squealing brakes of a hundred trains.

The boy part of me was telling me what to do. I had to get the monkeys back to the zoo.

I reared back with my front legs in the air. I waved them. My legs spoke louder than words.

'I am coming to get you, monkeys.' That's what my legs were saying.

The monkeys dropped to the floor. They landed in a squirming heap. In a flash they were scampering down the railway track with me after them. They were fast and so was I. It's amazing how quickly you can go with eight legs.

They were like a mob of sheep fleeing from the devil. One thing I knew about sheep was how they could break into groups and scatter if you chased them. Thank goodness the railway line was like a road keeping them together.

We belted down the track. On and on and on. The tribe followed The Big Pee but were finding it hard to keep up with him.

I kept chasing the monkeys and they kept running. After a long time they reached the road. I could see that they weren't sure what to do.

At that very moment I heard a sound. A welcome sound. I recognised the spluttering noise of Maggot's motorbike.

The fear fell from me. Just knowing that he was coming made me feel safe.

I felt myself begin to change. My extra legs vanished. I only had two. But they were both hairy.

The hairs began to vanish from my left leg. And then my right leg. It was working. Yes, two knobbly boy's knees.

I was me again. It was weird but I was kind of getting used to this now.

Maggot screeched to a stop and took off his helmet. The monkeys scrambled into the trees above.

'What's that?' I said. I pointed to something that looked like a rocket fixed to the side of his dented bike. The rocket thing had one wheel and a seat inside. And, and… it was full of bananas.

'A sidecar,' shouted Maggot with a big grin. 'My sidecar.'

'How did you find us?' I yelled.

Maggot tapped his nose. 'Followed the trail from the fruit stall,' he said.

At that moment another wonderful sound filled the air.

The noise was like a rushing stream. The stream became a river. The river became a thundering waterfall.

We both looked up as thirty motorbikes came to a stop.

15.

It was The Chief and Shark and Metal Mouth. And the rest of the bikie gang.

Thirty rough, tough, wonderful bearded bikies. They were led by Maggot's beloved Granny.

I couldn't believe it. Help had arrived.

Maggot handed me a helmet and patted the seat behind him. I climbed up and put my arms around his waist.

Maggot grabbed a banana and chucked it where the monkeys could see it. The monkeys fell like rain from the trees. They screeched and fought over one banana.

He nodded at the sidecar. 'One banana at a time,' he said. 'Take it easy.'

I grinned. Maggot had a plan. A good one.

He waved and the bikies moved into position.

They made two long lines with a passage between them. Granny took up the lead point at the front. Maggot fell in between the two rumbling rows of bikes.

Maggot pointed the way.

'To the zoo,' he yelled.

As we started to move, I reached over into the sidecar and grabbed a banana. I threw it out behind us. The monkeys sniffed. They looked. And then they came.

A squealing mob of monkeys scampered between the two lines of bikes. They ran behind the sidecar. I threw the bananas high in the air. Each one was grabbed and gobbled. Some monkeys took flying leaps like footballers going up for a mark.

It was working. The monkeys were following us. Maggot was a genius. I wasn't afraid. I was on top of the world.

We made our way along the main road and headed for the zoo. It was a fantastic sight. Me and Maggot, followed by a tribe of squabbling monkeys. And on each side a row of bikes stopped them from escaping. Right at the back I saw poor little Banana Boy all on his own. He wasn't getting any.

I threw the next banana straight to him. A powerful, strong throw. It bounced at his feet. He quickly grabbed the banana, peeled it and ate it before I could blink.

As we headed towards town I started to get

nervous. People would be watching us. Every eye would be looking. The thing I had always hated.

'Relax,' I said to myself. 'Relax.'

I knew that if I got nervous anything could happen.

Just the thought of all those people staring sent a shiver down my spine.

Finally we reached the edge of town. There was no sign of the zookeepers or the police. They were probably off in the bush somewhere. Following the wrong trail.

But hundreds of people lined the road and looked down from windows. They had heard we were coming. I saw the cameraman pointing his lens straight at me. And next to him was the woman with the microphone.

What if I turned into something while the world was watching? What if I turned into a banana? Was that possible? What if a monkey grabbed me and peeled me? And ate me?

There would be no coming back from that. I might end up as a small piece of monkey poo on the side of the road.

All of these thoughts swirled around in my head. But the thing that worried me most was the thought of the whole world looking at me.

I could sense the hot-and-cold feelings beginning to seep into my body.

I had to do something. Maggot slowed as we reached the crowd.

And gave me my chance.

I jumped off the bike and scampered behind some kids from school. No one even noticed me. Once again, I was What's His Name. I was safe.

Maggot was riding his bike but there was no one with him to throw out bananas from the sidecar. Some of the tribe were starting to fall behind.

Right at that very moment, a figure jumped onto the sidecar.

It was a monkey. Banana Boy. He grabbed a banana. But he didn't eat it. He threw it into the air. Then another and another. He was taking my place. Feeding the mob. The banana pile was growing slowly.

I fell in behind the crowd as they followed the bikes and the monkeys into the zoo.

Many of the other animals stopped to look as Maggot led the way. The crowd was quiet. Even the other animals seemed to be holding their breath.

Finally the bikies reached the monkey pen. They

switched off their engines and formed two silent rows leading up to the gate. No one wanted to frighten the monkeys right at the last minute. The zoo staff held fingers up to their lips. They knew that one wrong move would send the monkeys into meltdown.

The gate of the monkey pen hung open. There were hardly any bananas left. Oh, no. Banana Boy would never get them inside.

He threw a few more to the smallest monkeys. And then – oh, what? – there was only one banana left.

He waved it at the tribe from his perch on the sidecar. He was teasing them. Tempting them. He

hopped down and ran through the gate holding the last banana high above his head.

The mob followed. They ran after him. In the blink of an eye the tribe swept into the pen. They were all inside except one monkey – The Big Pee. He spat and hissed and didn't want to go. The tribe turned and looked at him. That's when I realised. He was telling them that he was the boss. He wasn't coming in. They had to come back to him.

Banana Boy gave a loud wail and waved the banana. The Big Pee screeched back. This went on for about twenty screeches. The monkeys' heads swivelled like people watching a tennis match.

Banana Boy stopped screeching and peeled the banana. He placed it at the gate. He gave one more screech and then all was still.

It was a test of will. If the boss took the banana he would not be the leader anymore.

Slowly, slowly, The Big Pee hopped into the pen. He grabbed the banana and gobbled it.

Banana Boy threw back his head and gave a mighty howl as Maggot closed the gate.

Banana Boy was the new boss. Yay. Maggot had pulled it off.

Maggot and the bikies were all surrounded by a crowd of cheering people. A girl ran out and stood next to Maggot. She put her arm around his neck and held out her phone. She was taking a selfie. I couldn't believe it. It was Gertag.

The cameraman and his helper saw what was going on and came over to talk to her. Gertag was going to be on TV.

Maggot spotted me hiding up the back and came over.

'Come on, mate,' he said. 'You're the hero here. Take a bow.'

I didn't want to take a bow. But I didn't want Gertag to take one, either.

'You posed with Gertag,' I said. He looked puzzled.

I shouldn't have been jealous. Maggot wasn't just friendly to me. He was nice to everyone. But it made me wonder. Where did I belong? Who was *my* tribe? I had to know.

I thought about my father again. Okay, he wasn't a hero like Maggot. But he would be like me. He was scared of spiders too. Maybe he even blended in when things got scary.

I started to push my way through the crowd. 'Where are you going?' said Maggot.

'To the park. I need to think things through,' I said.

'I'll see you at dinner,' he said.

I had forgotten about that. Why had Mum invited him to tea?

My heart grew cold. I knew they were going to talk me into seeing a doctor. Or a counsellor. No one had actually seen me change into something else. No one believed it. Including Mum and Maggot.

I had to find my dad. He would believe me.

'Yeah, see you tonight, Maggot,' I said.

I went home first, and put supplies in my backpack. Then I headed off towards the park.

It was past lunchtime and I was feeling hungry as I passed the two stone boys.

Two? The missing statue was back. Spouting water out of its mouth. They must have taken it away to fix it up. And now it was back.

The two statues were real. But one of them looked more real than the other. It was creepy. As if it was looking at me. I hurried on by and sat down on a park bench.

There was a row of bushes trimmed into shapes. There was a bush cut like a big ball. And another one exactly the same next to it. I started jogging towards it. But by the time I got there I found only one bush. This was weird. Where had the other bush gone?

Far off I saw two large dogs. Both the same. Exactly the same. Black with white snouts and white tails.

'Hey,' I yelled. The two dogs stopped, looked and then disappeared into the bushes. Only one ran out.

A few minutes later there was a rustling in the trees overhead.

Two identical possums were staring down at me.

The world was going crazy. Two statues, two bushes, two dogs and two possums.

It was a weird puzzle, but I had others to solve. All I could think about was finding my dad. I wanted him to come home. But he could be anywhere. And no one except Mum seemed to know where he was. And she wasn't telling.

I decided to go and look for him. Even if he was in Darwin. Or Tassie.

But no one would let a boy go on a plane. Or drive a car. Or ask questions about missing persons.

That was when I got an idea. A brilliant idea.

What if I was a man?

If I was a man I could go wherever I liked and do whatever I liked. I could even put a notice on Facebook. Or something like that.

What if, instead of trying *not* to change into something else, I did the opposite?

Could I copy something or someone on purpose? What if I made myself a man?

It was a good idea. But there was a problem.

I couldn't just sit next to a man on a bus and turn into a copy of him. He would freak out. I would probably get locked up.

I needed to practise on something else first.

That was when I heard barking.

'Woof, woof, woof.'

It was Sandy. He ran over to me and started jumping up. He loved me.

Just the thing. I could practise on him. If I could copy a dog, I could copy a person. Perfect.

I gave Sandy a few pats. Then I bent down and spoke to him.

'Sandy, boy,' I said. 'How would you like a friend? Someone just like yourself?'

I sat down on the park bench and held Sandy by the collar. Then I closed my eyes.

'Change,' I said to myself. 'Change into a dog.' I gave it everything I had. It was like trying to lift a train. That's how hard it was for my brain.

I thought about Sandy. Nothing but Sandy. Sweat ran down my face. I started to tingle all over.

I looked down at myself. Nothing. Just ordinary

legs. Ordinary boy's pants and jumper. Ordinary boy's hands and fingers.

Busting my boiler wasn't working. I needed to try something else.

Why didn't I do the opposite again? Maybe it would work for copying something. On purpose. Without being scared.

'Relax,' I said. 'Relax. Think of how much fun it would be to be a dog for a while.'

If I was a dog I wouldn't have to go to school. I would get pats on the head from a kind master. I could take a leak against a tree and no one would care. A warm glow started to wash over me.

Something was happening. I was changing. I was doing it on purpose.

I opened my eyes and looked down. Sandy was staring up at me with big eyes. He suddenly gave a yelp and pulled himself away. He ran squealing across the park.

I opened my mouth to call him back. But no words came.

'Woof, woof, woof,' I said.

I couldn't believe it. I was barking.

And I could see my own nose. I had a long snout with a rubbery bit on the end of it. I held my hands up to my face. It was all hairy.

Then I looked at my body and felt my head. What? Oh, no, no, no.

No, no, no, no, no. I had a boy's body and a dog's head. A dog with no ears. Just holes where they should be.

This was terrible. Horrible. I was half dog, half boy. It wasn't what I wanted.

I closed my eyes again.

Then I saw something else.

Maggot. Walking across the grass.

'Mate,' he said. 'I know that's you. That's a great mask. You've even scared Fearless. We have to talk. Your mum told me that you think you can turn into a bear. That's...'

He never finished the sentence.

I opened my jaws to speak.

'Woof, woof, woof,' I said.

Maggot grinned and gave my nose a little pinch.

I started to dribble onto him. Maggot looked at his wet hand. Then he stared at my long, flopping tongue. And the place where my ears should have been.

'Aargh,' he screamed. 'What's happened to you, mate?'

I started to relax a bit. He was a friend. He would understand. He would help.

'Relax,' I thought. 'Relax, relax, relax.'

Maggot just stared.

'Relax, relax, relax.'

Slowly I started to change. My rubbery nose disappeared from sight.

And I was normal again. This is when I realised how it all worked. I could turn the chameleon

effect on and off by relaxing. I was starting to get control over the whole thing.

Maggot rubbed his eyes.

'Did I just see what I think I saw?' he said.

I nodded.

'You were half dog?'

I nodded again.

Maggot sat down next to me and I told him the whole story. Everything. How I changed into a copy of something when I was scared. How I was once a spider. How I was trying to do it on purpose by relaxing. And how I was trying to find my dad. All that.

Maggot was hanging on to my hand. Squeezing it. Really tight. He banged his head with his spare hand as if he was trying to knock the whole crazy idea out of it. He was finding it hard to speak.

'You have to get help, mate,' he shrieked.

I looked at him.

'What sort of help?' I said.

'I dunno,' he said. 'Hospital maybe. Or a clinic.'

I just stared at him. I would never find my father if they put me in hospital.

'I'm a freak,' I said. 'I know that. There's no one else in the world like me.'

Maggot put his hand on my shoulder. He tried to calm himself. 'You are right,' he said. 'There is no one else like you. But you are not a freak. Every person is different. But there's always someone else somewhere who has got the same problem as you. Everything that has happened to you has happened to someone else.'

Maggot's words made me feel better. Someone else with my problem? That was good. But not what he said next.

'We need to get you into hospital. Let's go.'

'No,' I said.

'Yes,' said Maggot. 'It will be okay.'

He patted my head with a shaking hand.

'I don't want anyone to know,' I said. 'Not yet.'

'Come on, mate,' said Maggot. 'Now.'

I jumped to my feet.

'No,' I yelled. 'Not now. I have to find my father first. I'm not going to a clinic.'

I started to run across the grass. I could hear him yelling something, but I didn't take any notice.

In no time at all I was on the street.

I looked behind.

Maggot was after me. He turned and sprinted towards his motorbike.

I had to escape so that I could make myself into a man and search the country for my dad. I raced along the street looking for a place where Maggot wouldn't find me. Right then I saw it. Just the shot.

The town museum.

I ran inside.

I looked around the museum for a spot to hide. I couldn't see anywhere good enough.

There was a lot of stuff. A dinosaur skeleton. A human skeleton. Pictures on the wall. Old pots. Statues. Stuffed animals. Dead butterflies and insects. An old-fashioned plane hanging from the ceiling. A mummy inside an open coffin.

I looked around in panic.

'Blend in, blend in,' I said to myself.

Nothing happened. I stayed a boy. I heard the sound of hurried footsteps outside. Maggot was going to find me. And take me to see the doctor. And they would take me away from Mum. And I would never find my dad.

'Change, change, change,' I said.

Still nothing happened.

Then I remembered. Relax. Think of something nice.

I stared at a picture on the wall. Just a peaceful woman with a little smile. That was relaxing. I let my mind wander.

I thought of my dad. He was driving his Ferrari to the air force base. He was getting into his phantom jet plane.

It was a lovely thought. 'Relax,' I said. 'Relax.'

I continued to look at the painting of the peaceful woman. 'Blend in,' I said. 'Blend in. Change, change, change.'

Yes.

Something had happened. It worked. I had changed but at first I didn't know what I had turned into. I could move my eyes and nothing else.

MUMMY

People were moving along looking at things hanging on the wall. Two old ladies were staring at me.

'They're both the same,' said the tall one.

'They're both copies,' said the short one.

The two old ladies peered at me.

'Yes, very bad copies,' said the taller one. 'I've seen the real *Mona Lisa* in Paris. It's much smaller than these.'

They stood there staring. Then the short one walked around a bit. She kept looking at me as she went.

'Its eyes seem to follow you around the room,' she said.

The other one nodded.

'That's the sign of a good portrait,' she said. 'But they are still just copies.'

That's when I realised what had happened. I had copied the painting. I was a copy of a copy. I was a painting of the Mona Lisa.

I stared down from the wall as the two old ladies moved away.

Maggot burst through the door with a crash.

'Shh,' said the old ladies.

'Sorry,' said Maggot. 'But I've lost a kid.'

The old ladies nodded. 'We'll help you,' said the short one.

'Thanks,' said Maggot.

'What does he look like?' the other one asked.

'To tell the truth,' said Maggot, 'I don't really know. Could be anything.'

The tall one nodded. 'You never know what they will look like these days,' she said. 'My grandson has green hair and a ring in his nose.'

Maggot didn't seem to hear. He stood staring at the two statues. They held spears and shields. Two Greek Gods that looked alike. He went over to one of them.

'Is that you, mate?' he said.

'That's a sculpture, dear,' said the old lady next to him.

'Look at the eyes,' said Maggot. 'You can tell by the eyes.'

'I didn't know it worked for sculptures,' she said.

Maggot took off his leather jacket and hung it over one of the naked statues so that it covered the rude bits.

'Come on, mate,' he said to the statue. 'Calm down. Come back home and talk it over with your mother.'

The statue didn't answer. Maggot waved his hand in front of its eyes. It didn't move.

'It's not him,' he said.

Maggot took his jacket back and moved on. The two old ladies followed him.

He stopped in front of two stuffed Tasmanian devils. They had snarling mouths and sharp teeth. Maggot patted one of them on the head.

'Is that you, kiddo?' he said.

There was no answer.

He stared into its glass eyes. 'Don't look like that, mate,' Maggot said to the Tasmanian devil.

'Its eyes don't follow you around the room,' said the tall lady.

Maggot moved on to two lumps of brown stuff. He picked one of them up. Surely he didn't think that it was me.

'What is it?' said the short lady.

The other one read the label.

'Woolly mammoth poo,' she said.

Maggot hastily dropped the poo and moved into the next room, followed by the ladies.

'He might be in here,' he said.

But I wasn't in there. As soon as he was gone I started to relax. I willed myself to change back. And it began to work.

In no time at all I was myself again. I slipped off the wall and ran out into the sunshine.

As I jogged along my mind was in a whirl.

All I could think about now was my father. I had to find him. He would help me. But then a nasty thought entered my mind. Even if I did find him, he might not come home. He had vowed not to return until he had beaten his fear of spiders.

Behind me I could hear Maggot yelling. He had seen me.

'Stop,' he yelled. 'Stop, stop, stop.'

People in the street stopped and stared. They wondered what all the fuss was about. Maybe they thought I was a thief. All eyes were on me.

I started to pant. I went cold. Then hot. It was like I was drowning. I couldn't get enough air. But I fought it. I stayed calm. Even though I was running and people were looking, I didn't change. I was definitely getting control of this thing.

Maggot continued to shout. 'Mate. Stop. We need to talk.'

I had to escape. I had to hide.

I looked to the left. I looked to the right. I looked up.

Yes, yes, yes. The very thing.

A tall gum tree with twisted branches.

17.

I began to climb. Up, up, up.

I could hear Maggot's footsteps pounding on the footpath. Nearer and nearer.

I kept climbing. And climbing. Soon I was in the highest branches. If I fell, I would be history. Just a mangled mess on the ground.

Far below, the sound of footsteps died.

Maggot's voice floated up to me.

'Where are you, mate?'

He walked over to the letterbox that I had once copied. Not that Maggot knew about that.

Maggot spoke to it. 'Is that you?' he said. There was no answer, of course. He turned and searched the park with his eyes.

He looked up, and saw me.

'Don't move,' he yelled. 'I'm coming to get you.'

I clung to my branch as I stared down. Maggot began to climb.

'Don't look down,' he said. 'Just stay calm.'

'I'm okay,' I said. But I wasn't. It was a long way down. My head began to swim. 'Stay calm,' I said to myself. 'Stay calm.'

Maggot reached my branch. He stretched out a hand.

There was something about that hand being stretched out to me. A helping hand. You can't refuse a helping hand.

I reached out and put my hand in Maggot's.

And slipped.

And fell.

But Maggot had me. He hung on tight as I swung beneath him, high above the ground. He was sitting on a branch, holding on to me with one hand and a branch above his head with the other.

I dangled helplessly. I couldn't even get a word out. I wondered how long Maggot could last without letting me go. I could hear him panting and see sweat running down his face. My fingers were beginning to slip out of his grasp. I started to pant. I went cold. Then hot. It was like I was drowning. I couldn't get enough air.

Fight it, fight it, fight it. Relax and then then use it. Maybe I could copy something. A possum or a koala. But there was nothing to copy except trees and branches.

That's when I saw it.

The spider. The huntsman spider. The one that fell from the ceiling of the old railway station. I had been carrying it around all this time in my backpack without knowing it. The spider scampered along my arm.

I went cold all over. Don't change. Don't change. Maggot would fall for sure.

The spider ran onto Maggot's hand. He saw it. His face went white but he hung on to me desperately.

The spider began to crawl along his arm. It was moving really quickly. Up, up, up. Towards his face.

'Don't change, don't change,' I gasped.

I could see Maggot's eyes rolling. My eyes were rolling. There was nothing I could do. There was nothing Maggot could do to stop the spider's terrible journey. A shiver ran down my spine.

If Maggot let go with the hand holding me I would fall to my death. And if he let go with the other one we would both fall.

The spider ran onto Maggot's chest.

A strange look came into his eyes. They grew calm. I knew that he was fighting fear.

The spider was on Maggot's shoulders. Any second it would be on his face. It was moving like lightning. Maggot gave a squeal. Then he did the bravest thing I had ever seen.

He shot out a long, long tongue and grabbed the spider with it. He whipped his tongue back into his mouth like a frog eating an insect. Then he clamped his teeth together.

The spider was in his mouth. It was trapped.

I couldn't believe it. What a man. He had the spider in his mouth. I could see from his rolling eyes that the spider was probably walking around inside his cheeks.

Maggot suddenly spat the spider out into mid-air. It disappeared down below.

'Hang on,' said Maggot. He started to pull me up. His face was red. Sweat poured off him. I could hear him groaning. Slowly, slowly, slowly he pulled me up onto the branch next to him.

I was safe. And so was he. I could breathe again.

It took quite a while, but finally we climbed down to the ground with Maggot hanging on to me the whole way.

When we reached the ground Maggot spotted the wet, struggling spider on the footpath. For a moment I thought he was going to step on it.

But he didn't. It crawled off under a bush.

He gave me a great big smile. We just stood there on the footpath grinning at each other for ages and ages.

I didn't really know what to say. He had saved my life.

I nodded at the spider.

'My dad would never have been able to do that,' I said.

Maggot grinned. Then he said the most amazing thing. The magic words. The best words I had ever heard.

'Mate,' he said. 'I am your dad.'

18.

I just stood there like I was made of rock. Thoughts ran around inside my head so quickly that I could hardly catch them. Maggot was my father. He had just faced his biggest fear. He had caught a spider with his tongue. To save me.

I ran to Dad and hugged him. My best mate was my father.

'You're a hero,' I said to Maggot. 'No one else in the history of the world has ever caught a spider in their mouth.'

Maggot smiled and looked a bit shy. 'I won't say it was easy,' he said.

'I'm telling Mum,' I said. 'I'm telling her how you saved me from the spider. You saved my life.'

His smile grew even bigger. I could see that he wanted her to know how brave he was.

Our eyes met. We were both thinking the same thing. He was coming home.

For good.

'Give Mum a ring,' I said. 'Tell her what happened. Go on, go on. You can do it ... Dad.'

He took out his phone and tapped at the numbers.

'It's David,' I heard him say. He walked down the path. He didn't want me to hear. I didn't care. I was so happy. After a bit he came back.

'I'm going to get your mum,' he said. 'You wait here. I'll be back soon.' He jumped on his bike and was gone.

I stared around the park. Everything was lovely. Flowers gently dancing in the breeze. Birds chirping a last goodnight. Long shadows reaching the end of their daily journey.

Life was good. Maggot was my father. That meant that The Chief and Jaws and Metal Mouth were my uncles. And Granny was my great-grandmother. I had a lot of friends now. I didn't really need a friend my own age.

That last thought sort of clung inside my head.

It made me think. About the two statues I had seen. And the two bushes. And the two dogs. And the two possums. Almost exact copies of each other. What was going on?

I looked around for more pairs. But there were none. I couldn't work it out. But then the answer came into my head. I knew where to go.

I jogged back to the edge of the park. And stared up at the two stone boys.

Yes, two again. And one of them was a copy. It blinked. His eyes followed me around.

This boy knew more than me. He must have

had more practice. He had copied the bush and the dog and the possum. He could copy anything. And do it quickly. He was really good at it.

'It's okay,' I said to him. 'Watch this.'

I walked over to the letterbox. I closed my eyes and concentrated. Slowly, slowly I could feel myself changing. Then there were two letterboxes. And one of them was me.

Nothing happened. The two stone boys stood together without moving. I needed to demonstrate all I could do.

'Relax,' I said to myself. 'Relax.'

In a flash I was myself again. I was getting better and better at changing.

I looked at the stone boy. Nothing happened.

I needed something else to copy.

Yes. A seat.

I changed into a seat, but still nothing happened. The two stone boys didn't move. I didn't move either. I stayed a seat to see what he would do.

His lips trembled. His stone clothes came to life with colour. He was alive. He was a person. Just like me.

I relaxed a little and in a flash I was myself again. I didn't even have to try. It was like throwing a switch.

Our eyes met. He smiled. I smiled back. He had turned himself back into a real boy. He stepped down onto the path.

'You think copying a letterbox is good,' he said. 'Just watch this.'

In no time at all he changed and I found myself looking at...

Myself. The cheeky boy had copied me. It was like looking into a mirror. It felt really weird.

I laughed and laughed.

At that moment I heard the sound of engines. It was Granny and the whole bikie gang. Sandy sat behind The Chief with his tongue hanging out.

The gang parked their bikes and formed a great
circle with us in the middle.

Mum was there. Riding a bike. I couldn't
believe it. She was dressed in tight leather trousers
and a worn leather bomber jacket with the word
FIREBIRD on the back. Her belt was covered in
silver studs.

She gave me an amused grin.

'Yes,' she said. 'I can ride a bike too.'

She looked at the gang and then added, 'Better than any man.'

'You tell 'em, girl,' said Granny.

Everyone was so happy.

Mum and Maggot got off their bikes and walked towards me. Holding hands. I shook my head at the unbelievable sight. Mum and Dad hand in hand.

'This is so good,' I said.

Mum rushed forward and hugged me. And then Dad. The three of us just hugged, not talking. Everyone was smiling. None of them had noticed my new mate.

'You wanted me to get a friend my own age,' I said at last. 'And I have.'

They all looked at Stone Boy. Who wasn't made of stone anymore. They couldn't believe what they were seeing.

Especially Mum. She shook her head and stood there with her mouth hanging open. She looked at me. She didn't know which one was her son.

'Me,' I said.

Silence filled the air. Thirty-three pairs of eyes bugged out as they tried to make sense of two boys who were exactly the same.

All those eyes looking at us. I started to pant. I went cold. No, I didn't. I whacked a hand on the shoulder of the boy who was an exact copy of me.

I pointed at Maggot and whispered to my new friend. 'This is going to be fun,' I said.

He nodded his head.

'Let's do it,' he said.

Poor old Maggot.

You should have seen his faces.

All three of them.

AFTER ALL THAT

Well, that's just about everything that happened on that weekend.

After the second day things got better and better.

It was terrific having Magg—, er sorry, Dad back home. He was a great guy. And Mum was happy that she had her man back. Dad had proved himself by catching a spider with his tongue. But even if he hadn't we would still have loved him.

And Granny and the boys had come back with him. Me and Dad rode out to the caravan park and visited them every weekend. And Sand—, er, sorry, I mean Fearless was always waiting for us at the gate. After that we would get back on our Harley and go out to the zoo to visit Banana Boy, who was the best leader of monkeys in the world. The bikies, the family, and the animals. All of them are my friends.

It is a strange tribe. But it is my tribe.

And another thing. I can't believe this. Dad is a great cook. He can do a sausage on the barbie. And boil an egg. And make toast without burning it. And he hates stir-fry. But he pretends to like it and serves it up once a year on Mum's birthday.

Bad Bear still sleeps with me. And I still love him. And I don't care who knows it.

At school I put up my hand now and then. And I sit in the front with my new friend. We hang out together all the time. Stone Boy has gone through the same thing as me. But he started developing his powers before I even knew about mine. And he is better at it. I will tell you his story one day.

He can copy anything in a flash. Just by thinking about it. He is teaching me how to handle my powers. We keep them secret and only use them for good.

Well, mostly for good.

If you know what I mean.

And I did go to see a doctor at a clinic. He was a nice bloke and talked to me about my problems and had some good ideas. I told him about my abilities to change and all that but I could tell he didn't believe me. After about a year I got a bit sick of it and I copied his cat. He ran out yelling something about a tiger. Anyway, after that he told Mum and Dad that I didn't have to visit him anymore.

Gertag goes to see that doctor now. And it is doing her a lot of good. I saw her coming out of his office one day. It gave me quite a shock.

'Hi,' she said. 'It's nice to see you …

… Jeremy.'

Paul Jennings has written over one hundred stories and has won every Australian children's choice book award. Since the publication of *Unreal!* in 1985, readers all around the world have loved his books. The top-rating TV series *Round the Twist* and *Driven Crazy* were based on a selection of his enormously popular short-story collections such as *Unseen!* In 1995 he was made a Member of the Order of Australia for services to children's literature and he was awarded the prestigious Dromkeen Medal in 2001.

Craig Smith is one of Australia's most prolific children's book illustrators, with over 380 books published including Paul Jennings' Cabbage Patch Fib series. Craig's work over the last thirty years has been acknowledged in the Children's Book Council of Australia (CBCA) Book of the Year awards, as well as in children's choice awards around Australia. In 2011, Craig was awarded the biennial Euphemia Tanner Award, which recognised his distinguished services to children's literature and his encouragement of the joy of reading in children.

Also by Paul Jennings, with Andrew Weldon

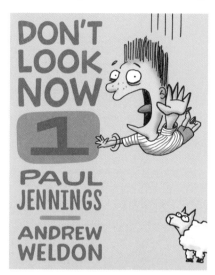

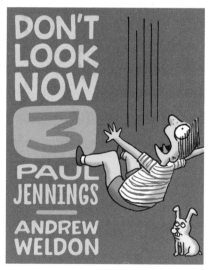
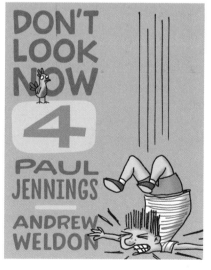